Praise for MAP OF IRELAND

"Stephanie Grant's voice . . . is the star of this well-written second novel. . . . The novel feels like a sustained heartbreak. . . . *Map of Ireland* is admirably ambitious, bold, and smart."
—*The Boston Globe*

"Race, sex, and community are the complicated and danger-ous pillars of the novel. Ann Ahern wants, literally, to climb out of her own skin, to be part of something larger than herself. This urgency fuels the novel and makes her unforgettable—unknowable but unforgettable."
—*Los Angeles Times*

"Stephanie Grant tells a rambling, rollicking good story that honors her own Irish roots."
—Kate Clinton, *The Progressive*

"Stephanie Grant expertly captures the confusion, angst, and insightfulness of a teenager dealing with race and sexual relations in a turbulent era."
—*Booklist*

"Edgy and erotic."
—*Publishers Weekly*

"A distinctive coming-of-age tale."
—*Kirkus Reviews*

"*Map of Ireland* is one those novels that unexpectedly fell into my lap virtually from nowhere and I was immediately hooked. I could not put this book down. Riveting, clear-eyed, spare, brutally honest, achingly poignant, Grant's story draws us into the Boston racial crisis brought to a head during the busing campaigns in the seventies. In the midst of this struggle, out steps Ann Ahern—one of the most disarming, haunted, and gorgeously conflicted narrators to come along in years. You will love this girl. You will fear for her, you will root for her. Ann Ahern will charm you; disarm you. She will enrage you, but she will never let you go."

—Alison Smith, author of *Name All the Animals*

"There is nothing that comes between the readers and what Stephanie Grant would like them to feel. *Map of Ireland* proves that she is an intensely graceful writer, capable of coupling vivid and conflicted characters with a profound sense of place."

—Christopher Rice, *New York Times*
bestselling author of *Blind Fall*

"In *Map of Ireland,* Stephanie Grant has written a novel of hard times that is a jagged jewel of perfection. With Ann Ahern, she has created a protagonist of fierce individuality, daunting irony, and always surprising courage—it is as if Charles Dickens had written a tomboy."

—Honor Moore, author of *The Bishop's Daughter*

"Winged words, new words: *Arrondisement. Nostalgie. Pyro-maniac. Penance* and *confession*. Language is Ann Ahern's and *Map of Ireland*'s magic charm. Making all new vocabulary that comes her way her own, including Irish-rooted hyperbole, this remarkable heroine defines herself through the words she acquires and 'becomes.' Drawing on foundational American myths about race and identity, Grant has written an unusual hybrid: a coming-of-age novel of ideas. This is smart work."

—Pearl Abraham, author of *The Seventh Beggar*

"Stephanie Grant's *Map of Ireland* is an openhearted, funny, and brave novel about the complexities of growing up in working-class Boston in the seventies. In Ann Ahern, she may have created the best tough-girl character since Scout Finch."

—Dana Spiotta, author of *Eat the Document*

"Stephanie Grant's fast-paced but beautifully turned new novel brings to troubled life once more the South Boston of the 1970s. It also brings to life Ann Ahern, a bright, wisecracking teenager who is part Huck Finn and part Holden Caulfield—as well as a maturing young woman with sexual longings for certain people who are both the 'wrong' race and the 'wrong' gender. Ann's freckled face, she's told, is a map of Ireland—but it's also a mask that Stephanie Grant strips to reveal a funny, sad, deeply sympathetic character."

—Mary Jo Salter, author of *Open Shutters* and *Sunday Skaters*

ALSO BY STEPHANIE GRANT

The Passion of Alice

MAP

of

IRELAND

A NOVEL

STEPHANIE GRANT

Scribner

New York London Toronto Sydney

SCRIBNER
A Division of Simon & Schuster, Inc.
1230 Avenue of the Americas
New York, NY 10020

First Scribner trade paperback edition May 2009

SCRIBNER and design are registered trademarks of
The Gale Group, Inc., used under license
by Simon & Schuster, Inc., the publisher of this work.

For information about special discounts for bulk purchases,
please contact Simon & Schuster Special Sales:
1-866-506-1949 or business@simonandschuster.com.

The Simon & Schuster Speakers Bureau can bring authors to your live event. For
more information or to book an event, contact the Simon & Schuster Speakers
Bureau at 1-866-248-3049 or visit our website at www.simonspeakers.com.

Designed by Kyoko Watanabe
Text set in Minion

Manufactured in the United States of America

1   3   5   7   9   10   8   6   4   2

Library of Congress Control Number: 2007045912

ISBN-13: 978-1-4165-5622-0
ISBN-10: 1-4165-5622-2
ISBN-13: 978-1-4165-5623-7 (pbk)
ISBN-10: 1-4165-5623-0 (pbk)

A portion of this novel appeared in a slightly different form as "The Map of
Ireland," excerpted in *Cabbage and Bones: An Anthology of Irish-American
Women's Fiction*, September 1997, Henry Holt, Caledonia Kearns, ed.

To my father, who has—always, always—had a bet on me.
And to my brother, who taught me to move toward the ball.

Geography is fate.

—Heraclitus

PART ONE

Southie Is
My Hometown

I was born on A Street,
Raised up on B Street
Southie Is My Hometown.
There's something about it
Permit me to shout it,
We're tough from miles around
We have doctors & trappers,
Preachers and flappers
And men from the old county down
Say they'll take you & break you
But never forsake you
Southie Is My Hometown.

—BENNY DROHAN

1

MADEMOISELLE EUGÉNIE WAS THE BLACKEST PERSON I'd ever seen. She was tall, with giant, almond eyes, and penciled eyebrows, and her hair sat high and stiff on her head, almost bouffant. On the first day of French class my junior year—which was not the first day of school—if you read the paper you know what happened the first day of school in South Boston in 1974; or even if you don't read the paper you probably know because it made the six o'clock news: There was film footage of the White parents lining Day Boulevard, throwing rocks at the buses, people we knew, Patty Flynn's ma—just the back of her head—but we recognized her from the bright red car coat. I can't remember any classes from that week, or the week after, just the yellow buses crawling up the hill: South Boston High sits up high on a hill, Telegraph Hill, and you can see the water from the top of the school steps; you can see cold, dirty, boatless Boston Bay. On the first day of French class that I *can* remember, the color shone off Mademoiselle Eugénie's skin, and I realized then, for the first time, that black had other colors in it.

She was bright, not shimmery like a lightbulb, but she lit up the room with her intensity and I wanted to look away but couldn't. We all watched her move around class the way French teachers do, darting between the rows of desks, up to the blackboard, then back to us, asking questions but moving before you could answer, so you had to crane your neck every which way to follow her complicated trajectory from your seat. I'm sure there's some scientific reason for it—like the part of your brain that learns foreign languages is wired to the part of your brain that cranes your neck—because they all do it, every freaking French teacher I've ever met.

But Mademoiselle Eugénie was the best. She was the best because she made you *want* to learn French. She made you want to *be* French. Or, at least, be another person. Someone not yourself. Someone, say, who moved her mouth in a particular way, like she was carefully sucking on a small egg, a robin's egg, maybe, although I don't think there are robins in Senegal, which is where Mademoiselle Eugénie is from, her family, I mean, before France: Senegal, West Africa. Someone who makes these wicked unusual, wicked un-American expressions because she's always sucking on that imaginary egg; someone who shows surprise, delight even, at sappy French sentences like, "My name is Ann Ahern and I want to go to the cinema." Someone who says *cinema* instead of *movies*.

My troubles began with several letters I wrote but didn't mail to Mademoiselle Eugénie. When I say, "my troubles," I mean everything that happened to me that first year of the busing. Everything I'm taking the time to tell you about here, now. Everything that has landed me in St. Joseph's Home for Girls. If I was a certain kind of person, I'd blame my troubles on the desegregation itself. I'd blame my being stuck here on those stupid yellow buses and the violence they seemed to bring.

But the truth is, my troubles started because I was too chicken to mail those letters and decided to burn them instead. The whole point of my telling the story is to tell the truth: It's the only way I know how to feel better anymore. I stopped going to church, not casually, not incidentally, but on purpose. I had what Sister Gail called a crisis of faith, but which was simply the realization that I had none—no flicker, no flame; you can't *fake* that—back when I was twelve. Even though I'm not a practicing Catholic anymore, I still need confession. They say once a Catholic, always a Catholic, and now that I don't partake of the sacraments, it's the confession itself that has become my penance.

My junior year in high school was a wild year, full of wild, what you might call, improbable change. It was the year when Nixon resigned and Ford became president; when Patty Hearst got kidnapped, then robbed a bank, and became *Tania*. We all watched her on TV, waving the machine gun. Also on TV, President Ford forgave Nixon. Then he partly forgave the draft dodgers. President Ford, it seemed, was full of forgiveness. Nobody else was. Nixon's pardon came three days before the first day of school in South Boston.

Sister Gail says the true meaning of the sacrament of penance is not forgiveness, but self-knowledge. She says it's through our sins, our trespasses, that we come to know who we truly are. I guess I'm trying to know myself, then, by telling this story; I'm trying to understand who my actions say I have become. My actions were this: I burned down the house of my friends. No one died, but someone went to jail because of what the police found inside. Remember, when people say, *burned to the ground*, they're usually speaking hyperbolically.

What, you think, because I live in the projects, I don't know that word, *hyperbolic*? Well, you're wrong. It's an Irish word. I inherited it from my family.

In three weeks, I turn eighteen and can leave St. Joe's, which, don't be fooled by the name, is a state facility for juvenile girls. In three weeks, I will have served out my full sentence, twenty months, my penance to the commonwealth. When I leave here,

I will be officially, legally, absolved by the state. But like most Catholics, practicing or not, I know that being absolved of wrongdoing and being absolved of guilt are two entirely different things. To tell the truth, the hardest part about not believing in God is having to live your whole life in the state of being not forgiven.

But now I'm getting ahead of myself.

Mademoiselle Eugénie came to Southie that year all the way from Paris, France. She was on an exchange program, except with teachers instead of kids. Mademoiselle Eugénie's other half was Mademoiselle Kit Kelly, our regular teacher, who'd taught at Southie High for years, since way back before the busing, when they needed one whole homeroom class for all the kids whose last names started with Mc.

My sophomore year, Mademoiselle Kit applied for the same program, and she made each of her classes do a special unit on the French capital. We all got maps and had to learn the different *arrondissements* by heart and I kept getting the left and right banks confused, which was stupid, I admit, but she took it like a personal insult, my inability to *feel* the difference between the two banks, like they meant anything at all to me, like they were anything but a bunch of squiggly lines on a page.

Every day in class, we ate Pillsbury Crescent Rolls that Mademoiselle Kit baked herself and we pretended that we'd just gotten back from the goddamn Louvre and were on our way to the goddamn Tuileries, which the whole class got in trouble for pronouncing Tool-eries. *Où est Didier? Didier est au Jardin du Luxembourg,* wherever on earth that is.

When Mademoiselle Kit's acceptance letter arrived saying she was definitely going to Paris, she made us all learn the French national anthem. The administration liked the idea so much, they made our decrepit music teacher teach the whole tenth-grade class the complicated French song. We had an assembly first period on the day Mademoiselle Eugénie arrived, which was the last day of school my sophomore year, the year before the busing began. Mademoiselle Eugénie had come to the United States early so she could have the entire summer to make the acquaintance of the city of Boston. That was how she talked: She didn't meet you, she made your acquaintance.

We must've sat in the assembly for two hours—not that anyone cared, we were just waiting for school to end, counting down each period bell—eleven! ten! nine! Later, we found out they'd kept her waiting while the headmaster called the exchange program to confirm that she was the right French teacher, the same one we were expecting, the very same Mademoiselle Eugénie Martine, from Paris, France. They made her sit in the outer office where you get sent when you're in trouble, a grimy little passageway with slippery plastic chairs and out-of-focus pictures on the walls of famous graduates who nobody's ever heard of and local politicians like Louise Day Hicks and Ray Flynn and Billy Bulger. Mademoiselle Eugénie sat, probably trying not to slide in her seat, chatting with Mademoiselle Kit, until the headmaster heard from three different people that the Black lady outside his door was definitely French.

Instead of singing *"La Marseillaise"* like we were supposed to, we sang "Southie Is My Hometown."

2

THERE WAS NOTHING PORNOGRAPHIC IN THE LETTERS to Mademoiselle Eugénie that I burned in a pile on our bathroom floor. They weren't exactly what you would call love letters, but they weren't exactly *not* love letters either. They were just descriptions, appreciations really, of the way Mademoiselle Eugénie moved, the way she spoke, the way she always seemed to be on the verge of an explosion of French words *not* in our vocabulary books.

It was late November, which in South Boston means cold, with the gray sky dropping down, like a low ceiling, over your head, and it's easy, if you tend that way in the first place, to feel a bit of despair, a bit of dread. I was burning the letters not because I was ashamed of what they said, but because, during the two and a half months in which I'd written them, I hadn't had the guts to send them. I could picture mailing them—I'd even licked the stupid ten-cent stamps—but I couldn't picture her receiving them. Every time I tried to imagine it, I got this hollow feeling in my stomach and throat, this feeling like I didn't have an esophagus at all, like my stomach was sitting right up under my chin.

I could picture her house. She lived in Jamaica Plain, which was on the other side of Roxbury, the main Black neighborhood. I knew the street, having ridden by on the bus once, not that I was freaking following her or anything, I just wanted to see the house, to see whether it looked like her, reflected her in some way. I'd had to take three different buses in order to go around, rather than through, Roxbury. Hers was a triple-decker, like a lot of houses in JP, a narrow, dark brown house, with cream trim, which seemed to be the standard colors for triple-deckers; there'd be a row of them, eight, ten identical houses right up against each other in that dirt dark brown and drab white, and you had to ask yourself if the people living there could tell their own depressing house from the next.

Mademoiselle Eugénie's house was narrow, but deep, almost a whole block deep, with three floors stacked like pancakes under a flat roof. At the end of a short cement walk was a mailbox, a triple-decker in its own right, three separate boxes with three of those little flags attached, two American, and one not French—it was black and yellow and red and green—I couldn't say, but figured maybe was Senegalese.

At first the house seemed impressive, almost grand—not cramped like where we lived—but then I saw it was seedy-looking, the ugly brown paint chipped, one of its gutters falling off. It was the kind of house where people stayed for a while, but didn't actually live, and I hated thinking about her being there, which is why I made the bus trip only once. I wanted to burn the letters because every time I got to the point in my mind where Mademoiselle Eugénie hustled down her short walk to the mailbox (she made you think of *action* verbs, Mademoiselle Eugénie did), every time I got to the point where she darted her hand into the box, her face went blank. Not her expression, but her whole face. She didn't have the almond eyes anymore, or that gently puckered mouth, or those drawn-on eyebrows that moved whenever she spoke. Nothing, just a blank, Black face and it scared me. Each time it happened, my stomach would crawl up my windpipe and just sit there, at the back of my throat, and I swore I could touch it, the slimy, acid insides, with my tongue. So I never sent the letters.

I hated not sending them. I felt like a coward not sending them, and the one thing I prided myself on being, the one thing everyone in the eleventh grade at South Boston High knew about Ann Ahern was that she wasn't a coward. So I had to burn the letters. To get rid of them, to get rid of the suggestion that I was a coward, when really, truthfully—you can ask anybody—I wasn't.

The fire I set in the too-small bathroom of our too-small apartment in the Old Harbor Projects was a modest fire, a neat fire, but Ma hit the roof anyway. I was something of a pyromaniac when I was a little kid, back before I'd understood the damage fire could do, back when I thought it had some separate—what's the word? Mademoiselle Eugénie taught it to us—*existential* value. The day my troubles began, Ma smelled the burning letters and bounded up the stairs two at a time. I remember the sound of her giant steps, her regular, hacked-up, smoker's breathing.

I had maybe thirty seconds from the moment I first heard Ma register the fire until the moment she flung the door open. (There are no locks on any of the doors in our house, not the bedrooms, not the bathroom.) She must have been sitting at the kitchen table because I heard her slight body hurl itself against the vinyl chair; I heard the chair scrape against the linoleum. I guess I was paralyzed though, or resigned maybe, because I didn't move. I didn't even try to put the fire out. I just sat there, on the edge of the tub, watching the letters burn, waiting for whatever was going to happen next to happen.

I suppose, if you wanted to get all psychological about it, you might say I wanted her to discover me there, burning those letters. I wanted her to find out, once and for all, that I was,

well, the way I was. There isn't a good word for it. It may surprise you to know, but everybody in Southie knew that I liked
girls only, and liked them that way. They knew since I tongued
Laura Miskinis in the ear on the first day of school in ninth
grade. Word traveled around Southie pretty fast—it's like a
small town, my neighborhood—word got passed like a bad
check, but the amazing thing was, nobody told my mother. Not
even my brother Hap, who took it the worst, who acted like it
was his problem to solve. I think the people who liked Ma, who
admired her, a woman on her own raising five kids, the people
who thought she had moxie, didn't have the courage to. And
the ones who hated her, my mother's enemies, so to speak
(everyone has enemies in a small town), the ones who said she
deserved what she got for bringing men around the way she
did, they preferred not telling her. They preferred pitying her
behind her back instead. They got a lot of enjoyment out of
that, instead.

But honestly, I don't remember thinking about any of this
at the time. I remember tapping the fire with the corner of my
sneaker, to let some air in; I remember watching the tiny
flames flutter, orange and yellow; I remember thinking about
how ugly the pink Housing Authority tile was, and how it was
the same in everybody's house that I knew; and I remember
feeling vaguely, yet, at the same time, intensely ashamed, when
suddenly the door flew almost off its hinges and into the room
and my mother was there.

Our bathroom's small: rusted-out sink, toilet, and half-tub,
in that order. There was no where to go. Ma and I looked at
the pile. Half the pages were ash, the rest were stained black
and brown by the smoke, their edges curling.

"Christ, Ann, what are you doing?"

I stood up. What can you say when your mother catches
you burning papers and whatnot on the bathroom floor? It
was pretty weird, even I knew that.

She brought her hands to her head. "I said, what are you doing?"

I shrugged and gestured to the dwindling pile.

"Are you trying to burn the house down?"

I shook my head.

"Answer me."

"No."

She's skinny, my mother. Not thin. Skinny, except for a pouchy stomach, which she blames on us five kids. One of those skeletal Irish ladies with freckles all over and red hair, but not exactly the color you'd want if you could choose. Kind of orange.

"Well, don't just stand there like an idiot." She pointed to the faucet. "Put the fire out."

For a second, I didn't move. The sink was right next to her. I had to step toward her to turn on the water. I didn't especially want to get close when she was mad like this. I knew she'd take a swipe at me. It's not like I'm some pathetic abused child or anything, but she wasn't above a healthy smack now and again, which is just what I got when I went for the sink, the back of her bony, freckled hand across my face.

"I could understand this when you were a kid, for Christ's sake. A little kid playing with matches. But I thought you were finished with that. I thought it was a phase."

I touched my stinging cheek.

"That's what Dr. McGraugh said. That it was a phase." She reached toward me, and I flinched, but she was just brushing the hair away from my eyes. "This is sick."

I shrugged and ran the faucet and cupped cold water in my hands, spilling it over the sorry pile. In fourth grade, I built fires against the south wall of Gate of Heaven during recess. When I got caught, the sisters asked me why, and I made the mistake of telling them the truth: I had thought the fire itself was on fire. I had thought the fire itself felt the terrible, consuming heat.

Ma folded her arms across her chest. "Can you tell me what's going on here? I really can't fathom it. I honestly can't."

"It's just. Some writing of mine. I didn't like it anymore."

"So you burned it?"

"Yes."

"Don't you think that's a little extreme?" Ma frowned in this exaggerated way. She had circles under the circles under her eyes. "Couldn't you have just thrown it away, like a normal person?"

Shrug from me. Exasperated sigh from her. Dr. McGraugh had also said that setting fires was more common, more normal, for boys.

"What's so terrible about the writing that you have to burn it? What's so bad?" She bent down. "What is it, letters?"

I grabbed her wrist and yanked the remains of my one-sided correspondence out of her hand. She lost her balance and had to step into the soggy ash pile.

"Shoot," she said, as she caught herself. She didn't use foul language, and she didn't like us to either. She wiped the sole of her shoe against the tile. The heels were so worn down the leather had started to peel. "They must be dirty letters."

"They're my letters, that's all."

She put her hands on her knobby hips and straddled the wet fire. She was wearing a dress, a faded paisley print with a clear plastic belt. Her stomach poked out beneath the belt. The last plumes of smoke went up there, between her legs. "I *know* they're dirty letters."

"Come off it, Ma."

"You can't kid a kidder, Ann." My mother and me are the exact same height, so she was looking right into my eyes. Hers are pale, pale, watery blue, the lashes so light, she doesn't seem to have any. She smirked, and her nostrils flared, and I could see she was thinking that I was a chip off her own, orange block, which really disgusted me because I wasn't.

"I'm going to count to three," she said. "And when I get to three, those filthy letters better be in my hand." She stopped smirking now and worked her thin lips into a line. She could be really cold when she wanted to. "One—"

"They're not filthy."

"Two—"

"Just because you're obscene doesn't mean everybody else is." This time, she hit me on the mouth.

I pushed past her, the burned letters in hand, and ran down the stairs and out of the house.

3

Ma joined ROAR at a church supper where Louise Day Hicks was the guest speaker. Mrs. Hicks was the founder of ROAR, which stood for Restore Our Alienated Rights, as well as Chairwoman of the School Committee, where she'd been fighting the busing for years. Louise was not an outsider, she was a daughter of Southie, plump and grandmotherly in a stern sort of way, her father a judge with a street named after him, Day Boulevard. After Indian pudding had been served in the basement of St. Monica's, Mrs. Hicks had said: "If the suburbs are so interested in solving the problems of Blacks, why don't they build subsidized housing for them in their own towns, in their own neighborhoods?"

A week before, Ma had argued with her sister about the busing, and Aunt Helen had made her feel prejudiced, which Ma didn't consider herself; it was low class to be prejudiced and Ma wasn't low class, despite her—our—circumstances. And when Mrs. Hicks said that about the people who lived in the suburbs, Ma realized the liberals who'd moved out of the city to live in Milton and Newton and Needham, and all the other towns along Route 128, the expressway that circled the city like an expensive belt, she realized they all were hypocrites. Why, they'd left the city precisely so they wouldn't have to deal with Blacks. Not in a million years would Aunt Helen have let my cousins go to school in Roxbury and Ma knew it, but Mrs. Hicks had said it first, had spoken Ma's suspicions out loud, and because there was no sin worse than hypocrisy in Ma's book, she became a staunch supporter of Mrs. Hicks.

On the first day of school, Ma kept us home because she was afraid of the violence. We sat around the TV—all the stations interrupted their regular programming—and she clucked disapprovingly at the tube and said it was embarrassing, White parents putting little colored kids in danger; wasn't that what the antibusing movement was about in the first place, protecting our children, our babies? Ma never used the word *nigger,* she said *colored* or sometimes *Black,* and she pretty much approved of the Reverend Dr. Martin Luther King, Jr., she thought all the segregated bathrooms and bubblers down South were completely unfair, completely un-American.

Besides, out of four kids in the school system (Hap had just graduated), only one got bused, which was better than most families, which was pretty good percentagewise, except that Timmy was Ma's favorite, her baby, for years it had been the twins, but now Maura and Margaret were in junior high and kept to themselves and laughed too hard at things that weren't funny, and Ma was exhausted by their secrecy. Plus, boys were naturally less critical of their mothers, she said.

So, after a month of putting Timmy on the bus for Roxbury every morning, after a month of watching chaotic protests that had won the people of South Boston exactly nothing, Ma joined one of the Mother's Marches, which were supposed to be peaceful, mothers only, no fathers, and no kids allowed. At each march, the women walked to the school and knelt in front of the police, the Tactical Patrol Force, and recited the rosary together, out loud. Defenseless mothers— they were nobody's fools—against well-armed police—they knew what it looked like, devout Catholic mothers kneeling and praying: *and blessed is the fruit of thy womb, Jesus.* That's sixtysome prayers, outdoors, on the ground.

One day, toward the end of October, the mothers got restless and tried to enter the school. Which was against the law—another decree from Judge Arthur Garrity, the same judge who'd ordered the busing: no parents in the building during school hours (he was a tyrant—a tyrant!—who ruled by decree). Ma was in the front line of mothers. Hap and me and Timmy and the twins stood watching from the far side of G Street. We were at the bottom of the hill, stuck behind police barricades, the side streets dropping down and away behind us, the silver water suddenly visible, flashing like sunlight between the houses to our left. I hoisted Timmy up, onto my shoulders, so that he could see.

Maybe two hundred mothers knelt down in the street, heads bent, before the cops. The TPF weren't regular police; they were big, beefy guys in leather jackets and riot helmets with Plexiglas visors. Instead of guns, they carried long wooden batons and stood in military-style rows between the women and the school. It was a cold, damp October day, an east wind whipping off the water and up the hill; our mothers' flimsy cloth coats flapped in the wind. We listened to their voices rise and fall together, fall and rise. The only other sound the squawk of police radios. A few hundred of us clogged the side streets that led up to the high school. The TV crews got stuck behind the blue barricades too; one of the cameramen almost knocked Timmy off my shoulders as he worked to get a better view.

When the mothers finished the rosary, they stood. It took them a minute; they'd been kneeling for more than half an hour, and you could see the stiffness in their ankles and knees. Two ladies stumbled as they rose. It gave me a tingly, hyper sort of feeling, watching them struggle. One of the two—she'd worn a check skirt, taupe panty hose—her kneecaps trickled blood. All the reporters wanted a picture of that. They jockeyed for position behind the barricades. For a split second, I could see how strange we must have looked to outsiders: the bloody kneecaps, the black and silver rosary beads.

When the women plowed into the police line—heads lowered, arms linked—the police didn't hit anyone, but they shoved back. They held the wooden batons horizontally against their chests, and they pushed almost gingerly; they weren't swinging; they pushed almost reluctant; and three or four of the mothers were knocked to the ground. I remember straining, looking for Ma. Timmy's weight was on my shoulders pressing down, and I was pushing up, practically out of my sneakers, searching for Ma's orange hair, and then, there it was, falling, falling, like a flame. I put Timmy down. My throat closed. But then the crowd of spectators surged forward, into the barricades, and all of a sudden there were tons more cops—cops on horses, cops on motorcycles—and we couldn't get anywhere, couldn't move forward. I picked Timmy back up. I could smell the horses. Timmy was six years old, maybe forty-five pounds. I felt trapped. I looked around for Hap and the twins. In less than a minute, we'd been separated. I rubbed Timmy's head and told him everything would be all right. I backed my way out, carrying him on my hip, like a baby—I hadn't carried Timmy that way in years, couldn't remember the last time he'd let me. I lugged him all the way back down the hill to Old Harbor.

That night, when she got home, still limping, Ma was exhilarated. She said it was the most important day of her life. She'd been arrested, charged with a federal offense, though she couldn't remember which one. Later, after Hap had gone out to throw rocks at the police (he was in the SBLA, the South Boston Liberation Army, which was made of kids too militant for ROAR), and Timmy and the twins had gone to bed, Ma stood in the courtyard with the other mothers, talking. I listened from the single concrete step in front of our building. Ma used her whole body to talk—arms and face, of course, but hips and bum too—everything moving. Her voice was low, rich-sounding from the cigarettes. At one point, she pulled down her pants and showed them the ugly scrape.

4

On the day that I fought with my mother, I took a city bus to Northeastern. I wanted out of my house, but also, out of my neighborhood. South Boston is what they call a peninsula, which means water on three sides, which means you have to make an effort to leave it; the T doesn't go there, only runs alongside, at the base of that fourth, landed side. In other words, you have work to reach the rest of the city, which some people in the Town never do. I sat in the back of the bus and looked at my fat lip in the mirror that hung above the exit. The mirror was round, tilted at a funny angle, with thick glass that distorted the reflection. My whole face, not just my lip, looked woozy, inflated.

Usually, when I went to Northeastern, I went to spy on the college girls. Freaky suburban girls who didn't suspect a thing. In Southie, since word got out about me and Laura Miskinis, I couldn't look at a girl very long without her noticing. And when she did, that meant a stupid fight with her stupid boyfriend, or brother, or what have you. I found myself trying not to be in a fight almost every other week. People liked to say that my neighborhood was close-knit, everyone looking out for everybody else, which was precisely what they liked, and precisely what I didn't. At Northeastern, I felt more free. The students were into their own thing, were live and let live.

The campus was a jumble of buildings set too close together, some old and covered with ivy, others ugly steel and concrete. I walked down a narrow passage between two ancient brick buildings and came to a wide open space called the Quad. The first snows had been shoveled into dingy clumps and a million feet had trampled over the frozen ground leaving this gray slush. There were concrete paths but nobody seemed to follow them. I liked the Quad, even in winter; the openness was like a secret kept from the rest of the city. That afternoon was cold and rainy, the kind of rain that makes you wish for snow. I was wearing a dungaree jacket, my brother Hap's, pretend lamb's wool around the collar, which was soft when he bought it, but had gotten stiff and scratchy after washing, the white tufts freezing into crusty peaks. It wasn't anywhere near warm enough. I walked with my shoulders tight together, my tongue tracing the edge of my swollen lower lip.

I passed two girls in gunnysack dresses; their long skirts dragged wet and heavy on the slushy ground. Water stains climbed up the plain material, past their knees, disappearing under their coats, but the girls didn't seem to care. Most of the students were like that, oblivious, they wore whatever they pleased, elephant bells, ugly gunnysack, or tie-dyed anything, which was way out of fashion. It was as if they didn't realize that times had changed, and it wasn't the sixties anymore, and I had the urge to tell those two, but they didn't once pick up their heads. I could see the outline of their thick thighs beneath the wet dresses.

Honestly, I was watching the college girls more out of habit than anything else. I was killing time. For maybe half an hour, I walked around campus, nursing my fat lip, trying not to feel sorry for myself. Then I turned onto Huntington Avenue and walked along the trolley line to the Flick, to the old-time movie theater where my best friend, Patty Flynn, worked.

Flynn sold tickets in the tiny booth outside the movie theater because her boss thought a fat girl selling candy would discourage purchases. The other workers rotated jobs, but not Flynn. She was always in the booth. When I reached the window, she hopped off her stool and opened the door and let me in, which was completely against the rules.

"What Hap do to your mush?"

I shook my head. "It was Ma."

Flynn sat back down to sell tickets. It was cold in the booth. She wore black knit gloves with the fingers cut off. "Your mother sure packs a wallop." By her feet was an electric heater. Outside, a long line for the double feature: *A Streetcar Named Desire* and *On the Waterfront*. The heater gave off a bitter, burning smell. "Why she hit you?"

"Search me."

"I swear, the skinny ones are meaner."

I touched my swollen lip. There was dried blood. Flynn was my only female friend after word got out about me.

She sniffed. "The guinea never hits us hard."

She was the youngest of six, had five brothers, black Irish, everyone said because of their dark hair and skin, but it was really that the mother was Italian. Flynn and me never talked about my liking girls. We hardly talked period. We played basketball, that's what we did together, since fourth grade; we could pass to each other without even looking. "Seriously," she said, "why she hit you?"

I shrugged even though I was standing behind her, and she couldn't see the gesture. "I was burning some stuff on the bathroom floor."

Flynn turned around. She tossed her hair out of her eyes. It was dyed blonde, the color of Karo corn syrup, the wings layered in two fans away from her face. Flynn was meticulous

about her appearance except for being fat. "I thought you out-
grew that shit."

I shrugged again.

"What were you burning?"

"I don't know. Personal stuff."

There was a knock on the glass. A Black with long hair and
a Jesus beard—they had everything, *every*thing here!—was
waving his money around.

Flynn swiveled back to the window. She always went extra
slow when someone was in a rush. Now she pushed each dol-
lar through the window slot one at a time. The Black kept tapping the glass. "You don't know what you set fire to?"

"Some letters, I guess."

"Who to?"

I could feel the words forming in my throat. "A friend."

"You don't have any friends."

Flynn sold eight tickets in a row. It was mostly Northeastern students in their weird outfits. I watched her hands. On the
back of her wrist was the Southie dot, just visible beneath her
cut-off gloves; she'd gotten the tattoo two years ago, but I'd
refused. I wished she would talk about something else, and she
did. She said, "Mike McGuire came by here looking for a
senior citizens' discount, can you believe it?"

"Yes."

"What elephant balls."

"You didn't let him?"

"No way. I told him he could ask me in school, in front of
his friends."

"What he say?"

"You know he's in the SBLA?"

"He wears that stupid green armband in school."

"We sat across from his mother at the ROAR meeting last
night. I'm thinking of telling her that Mike breaks the second
commandment when he cums."

"Jesus, Flynn."

"That's just what he says. 'Jesus, Flynn. Christ, Flynn. Mother of God, Flynn.' I was starting to feel like a member of the Holy Family."

"That's exactly how I think of you."

Flynn didn't have any female friends at school either, despite being a member of ROAR. She was fat and a slut, which went against people's sense of propriety.

"Can I ask you something?"

Flynn swiveled around.

"Don't you miss playing ball?"

"Try asking something you don't already know the answer to."

"All right." Flynn was not sympathetic. That was the main thing about her personality. She was not interested in other people's feelings. "What about Mike McGuire? Do you ever wonder—?"

She shook her head. "Elly's inside."

"Yeah? Ushering?"

She turned back to selling tickets. "Selling popcorn. You want a senior citizens'?"

5

THE FIRST TIME THE TWO BLACK GIRLS PLAYED BALL with us, the headmaster escorted them to practice. The center walked incredibly slow, I'll never forget, like a little kid being dragged to school, every step a protest. Her name was Rochelle; she was tall and slim, pretty dark-skinned, with a big, mushrooming Afro. You couldn't miss her. Devonne, the guard who eventually replaced Flynn, was shorter, thicker, her hair braided like train tracks tight across her scalp; she slowed her pace to match Rochelle's and wore this unbelievably bored expression like she was doing us all a favor. They both wore brand-new Southie High sweatshirts, the traditional gold and blue. We stopped playing and watched the three of them cross the gym. I swear it took forever. Flynn was digging her elbow into my side, and I realized I knew exactly what she was thinking: Those sweatshirts were so strange, so unnatural on the girls, they looked like costumes.

Then the two Blacks stood each with her weight on a single leg, each examining the cuff of her new sleeve, while the headmaster asked our coach, Was it true that the day before he'd refused to let them play? Red-faced, stuttering, Coach Curry explained how those two had come incredibly late, and he'd already assigned the teams, so they'd had to warm the bench, which apparently they didn't like—they were starters at Roxbury High, big stars—but which was the rule for everyone here; Coach Curry never broke it.

The headmaster nodded in this earnest way like he understood, then said, How, during these difficult times, we all had to make an extra effort, yadda, yadda. Which meant Rochelle and Devonne could do whatever they pleased, break any rule, it didn't matter. Coach Curry knew it, and so did we, and he looked at us like, *I tried my best, but my hands are tied,* and we loved him, loved him, for choosing sides.

When Rochelle stepped on the court, a look passed over her face that I thought maybe was relief, but I couldn't tell, it disappeared too quickly; then she trotted, no hurry, to the far basket. She was halfway there when Coach Curry blew the whistle and Devonne made an inbound pass almost the entire length of the court, and Rochelle reached up with only one hand, barely tapping the ball, and redirected it toward the basket. She took two steps, still in control, still relaxed, and went in for a layup.

When she was back on the ground, Flynn said, "Isn't anyone going to call her for traveling? Doesn't anyone here have the balls to call that nigger for traveling?"

We all froze in place and looked at Coach Curry, who had a different expression on his face now—not conciliatory, not understanding. He was staring at Rochelle, trying not to smile, trying not to show his excitement. Our regular center, a flat-footed Polish girl who rarely scored, bent down to tie her sneaker; she was ashen. Coach Curry wiped the sweat off his upper lip. "During these difficult times, we all have to—" then he swallowed his words. And cleared his throat. "Plus, another outburst from you, Patty Flynn, and you'll be warming the bench."

But Flynn was already skulking toward the lockers. She tore her own, ancient Southie sweatshirt off and threw it on the floor of the gym. "Fucking traitor," she said, under her breath, but loud enough so that everyone could hear. "Fucking Benedict Arnold."

Me, I tried not to think about the busing. Mostly, I tried to put it out of my mind. Aside from this—the awful inconvenience of losing Flynn—I found it mostly embarrassing. For instance, that fall, George Wallace came to show his solidarity with the people of South Boston. I went with Ma to hear him speak, and I remember feeling incredibly ashamed. The paralyzed governor in his drooping wheelchair. That stupid-sounding drawl! I kept staring at his useless legs. He was not handsome, like the Kennedys. He was shriveled, old. His suit seemed two sizes too big. When our own Governor Sargent called out the National Guard to protect the schools, he said the whole nation had its eyes on Boston. And you could actually feel that at the demonstrations, you could feel that attentiveness. But I worried, if the whole country was watching, what exactly did they see?

Take Elly, for instance, Flynn's only friend at the Flick. She was from the suburbs. She went to Boston University—she studied nursing—and she knew Flynn and me were from South Boston. What I didn't know was: Did she think we were low class? Poor? Did she think the backs of our necks were red?

The first thing Elly did when she saw my busted lip was get me a cup of ice. She was working the concession stand in the Flick's old-time lobby, three antique candy counters arranged in a triangle. "Oooh," Elly said. "Oooh, oooh. What happened?" She leaned forward, stretching her soft belly out over one of the glass counters, and handed me a wax paper cup. She smelled of popcorn. "Suck on these," she said.

I put two of the miniature cubes against my lower lip and winced from the cold. It was distracting instead of soothing. Elly was way into this Victorian-Vampire look; she had dyed blue-black hair and a big, round, powder-white face.

"Better?" she asked.

I nodded, and she smiled again.

"Does it still hurt?"

"Not really."

She was not pretty, but not ugly either. Elly had a wide mouth with a lot of small, square teeth. They were about the size of the mini ice cubes I was sucking on. She reached up and touched my lip. "Well, at least it's a neat color."

Elly had never touched me before, but I didn't pull back. It felt pretty regular, like a sister's touch, not electric or anything, which I admit I had more or less imagined because of having a crush on her.

"Want more ice?"

"Uh-uh."

"A tonic maybe?"

I shook my head.

She pointed to where Ma had slapped my cheek. "You're going to have a shiner there."

I didn't know what to say. I wanted to tell her she would make a good nurse, but I just stood still, breathing in the popcorn smell and looking at her hand up close, then at the white White arm, and I started wondering in that way I have of getting distracted at the precise moment when I should be paying the most attention, I started wondering why it was that the people with the whitest skin in the first place usually went into the Victorian-Vampire thing, so the powder they used, the talc or what have you, was pretty much beside the point. My eyes sort of trailed off while I was thinking this, I was making a mental note to ask Flynn about it, and my eyes wandered all the way up Elly's arm, past her elbow to her shoulder and neck, and before I realized it, I was staring down her blouse, at her cleavage, which she had a considerable amount of.

When I raised my eyes, Elly was looking straight at me, watching me stare, and I felt bad instantly and turned my head away, but obviously, obviously, it was too late. I glanced around. Flynn was still in the ticket booth.

I knew you weren't supposed to stare at girls that way anymore. I watched the news, read the paper. I knew how it was degrading for girls to be looked at like that, and I hadn't meant to degrade Elly—it was the last thing I wanted!—but her boobs were right there, practically falling out of her black blouse and onto the glass case; I even saw the brownish pink edge of one of her nipples, so far the only bit of color on her body, which made me start to sweat. I felt damp under my arms and at the nape of my neck.

Elly seemed as uncomfortable as me. She pulled back from the edge of the glass counter, then knelt down and reached into the case for Junior Mints. I was disappointed because I liked Milk Duds not Junior Mints and Elly knew this, but I think she just grabbed the first box she came in contact with, eager to get me out of there as quickly as possible.

"I've got customers," she said, her eyes still on the glass case, and turned to the next counter in the triangle.

Now, it occurs to me that I might be giving a false impression. I mean, here I am telling a story, which is basically the story of my feelings for Mademoiselle Eugénie, and what happened as a result of them, and now, lo and behold, I'm talking about some other girl, an altogether different person. Like I said before, I did have a crush on Elly, but it was not at all like the feelings I had for Mademoiselle Eugénie. I had this awareness of Elly, this pleasant, physical recognition of her, which made me conscious of my own body whenever we talked. Like in those TV movies when there's a kid inside a robot moving levers to make the robot arms extend and the robot knees flex, and things go pretty smoothly until the kid gets nervous and pulls the wrong lever and the knee comes up for a handshake and the fingers open when they're supposed to close. It's like there's a second self inside your regular self and it's constantly

going, "Now take the ice cubes from Elly. Now smile." It's a per-
petual monologue inside your head, which is why it can be hard
to make conversation with the girl you're actually talking to.

When I spoke to Mademoiselle Eugénie, there was no extra
monologue in my head, only pure thoughts and ideas, and it
felt like what I'd always wanted to happen at Mass, but never
did. I figured I was in love with Mademoiselle Eugénie because
my feelings had nothing to do with bodies, and probably that
was what the libbers were getting at in the newspapers; if you
really loved a girl, you didn't think of her in pieces, you
thought of her as a whole.

This was what was running through my mind when I sat
down and watched the heavy gold curtain rise and bore witness to—but didn't actually see—the previews and ate Junior
Mints and tried to forget what had just happened between Elly
and me. The Junior Mints weren't so bad. I held them in my
mouth and let them melt. My tongue felt cool and thick at
once. I was hoping Elly and Flynn wouldn't come into the
movie theater when they were through with their jobs, like
they usually did. Elly especially had the capacity to watch
movies over and over again, which was partly why she was so
interesting to talk to. She'd watched some movies so many
times, she saw them in this unique way, which reminded me of
how much I liked her, which reminded me of how bad I felt
for blatantly staring at her boobs, and then *Streetcar* came on,
and Marlon Brando filled the screen.

He was huge and handsome. I wasn't prepared for how
handsome he was. He moved like falling water, graceful, curving around furniture and people, filling up the space between
things, then all of a sudden hard and forceful and you'd better
get out of the way. He crashed in and out of the two ratty
rooms where they lived in the French Quarter of New Orleans.
There was only a curtain separating the two rooms. You
thought any minute he was going to tear it down.

He loved his wife, Kim Hunter. They went at it every chance they got until the sister showed up. They had the wicked intense hots for each other. But he hated Kim Hunter too. You could tell that, even when he was touching her, or wanting to, you could see the disdain. He blamed her for something he felt, but couldn't say. He was cruel to the sister, Vivien Leigh. You could see he wanted to strangle her. It was everything he could do not to.

I felt this feeling which I'd had before, but which still seemed new. I was attracted to the man instead of the woman. I got suddenly hot in the movie theater, suddenly aware of the texture of my seat cushion. I touched the red velvet in the opening between my thighs and felt horny and embarrassed. Marlon Brando was beautiful. His big, fat lips curved like a girl's. He wore a sweat-stained T-shirt practically through that whole goddamn movie. It was hot there, in New Orleans, you could tell, it was hot and humid. That freaking T-shirt was stuck to him. You could see his pectorals and his nipples pushing like breasts against the dingy cotton. Not that he looked faggoty, not at all. Or girlish. He looked hard, but not too hard. Full is more like it. The way a grown woman is full, meaning fleshy, but wholly masculine at the same time. Well, maybe not wholly. Not 100 percent. I'm sure you're thinking I'm confused. This girl is confused. But he was like that on the giant screen, looming and confused himself, one moment womanly, the next manly, and I found myself thinking about him instead of the women.

Now Vivien Leigh was who I'd normally be focused on; even playing that old Blanche DuBois she was sexy, even washed up, even pathetic like she was in those faded flouncy dresses, you could still feel the sex coming off her. She had an appetite. But as much as I admired her tired sexiness, I couldn't take my eyes off Marlon Brando. He wore these amazing pajamas. They were poor, but somehow he'd gotten hold of these beautiful broad-striped, black-and-gray pajamas.

Near the end of the movie, Marlon Brando got mad at Vivien Leigh. It looked as if he really was going to strangle her. Then it looked like he might do something worse. She broke a bottle in half—in Southie, what we call a nigger knife—but he managed to get it away from her. He pinned her arms back, his striped muscles blooming against her bleached-white Southern skin. I was staring at his arm next to hers—it was like silk against paper—only he was the silk, she was parched, feathery—I was staring at how beautiful and how cruel he was, and then I realized I wanted to be him.

It made me feel strange to realize this. Kind of light-headed. It's not that I wanted to be a guy. Mostly I hated guys. They were stupid beyond belief. When they weren't beating up on someone, when they weren't being complete assholes, they were incredibly boring. But I definitely wanted to be Marlon Brando. My stomach hurt, I wanted it so bad. I wanted to move like him, slippery and forceful at once. I wanted to grab Vivien Leigh. It made me ashamed, but it was true. I wanted her to look at me the way she looked at him. Kind of fearful. I wanted her to whimper.

By the time *Streetcar* ended, I was feeling pretty lousy. He raped her in the end. They didn't show it. They didn't show stuff like that in movies back then, but if you were paying attention at all, you figured it out.

At that point in time, I hadn't had sex with a girl yet, though I thought about it a lot. I imagined it most nights before I went to sleep. I pictured it in my mind's eye, and I touched myself. It was the same every time: We were at Carson Beach. Usually the girl had all her clothes off. Usually it was somebody I knew, Laura Miskinis or one of her friends. Who- ever she was, she had nice boobs. Not humongous, like in those men's magazines, but big, bigger than your hand. Plus round and hard. I'd close my eyes and put my hand between my legs, only I'd pretend I was touching this naked girl. I imagined my other hand holding me up so I could get a good look at her bare skin. Every night I could feel the grainy sand under my fingers on Carson Beach. To tell the truth, sometimes I wished I had a guy's thing just so I could free up one hand and touch her boobs. Sometimes, right when I came, I pictured a guy's thing inside me. It was pretty confusing. I mean, definitely confusing. But I liked the feeling of something inside me, something to grab on to. I figured I'd figure this all out when I had a real-live girl, a living, breathing one, underneath me.

I was sitting in the dark, not particularly watching the second movie, *On the Waterfront,* wondering if there was something wrong with me for wanting to be Marlon Brando, when Elly and Flynn sat down on my right-hand side. The seats at the Flick were big, wider than usual, with the rows spaced far apart so there was plenty of leg room. But when they sat down, Elly next to me, Flynn next to Elly, it got very close. Humid like New Orleans. I started to sweat. I took my elbow off the armrest between Elly and me. I nodded at her, then at Flynn who offered us popcorn from the big bucket she held in her lap. I shook my head no, then turned back to the movie. I could feel Elly next to me, not eating popcorn either. For what seemed like a minute I held my breath and stared at the screen. Just when it seemed safe enough to breathe, Elly put a hand on my thigh.

6

Patty Flynn's father took off at about the same time as mine, but for different reasons. Her dad was a bookie who spent his days in the Quencher Tavern or Shannon's or Dot's Donut Shop on West Broadway; that was his territory. When Flynn was in the fourth grade, he went to jail because he refused to testify about the people he paid rent to. There was a big crackdown on betting; the district attorney had all the bookies arrested and some of them talked, but Flynn's father didn't and he was put in prison for what they called criminal contempt of court. His lawyer said it was a sham and that Flynn's dad would have to be released, but then he got in a fight with some guy in jail.

It was hard to picture Flynn's father in a fight; he was one of those unobtrusive little Irishmen, the type who always had his head in the paper and drank his beer quietly and never fought with anyone, not even Mrs. Flynn. He was a good bookie, people said, because you never noticed him coming or going, he was just there when you wanted to play the football card or place a bet on a promising horse with an Irish name at Suffolk Downs. People said he'd been a jockey in his youth, which was excellent training for a bookie and the best kind of physical work for a small man.

He was in prison in Concord, a minimum-security prison, which wasn't far; Flynn could take the train, not the T but the Commuter Rail, to see him on weekends. But she didn't. It was fucking depressing, Flynn said, seeing him grow smaller month by month. Patty's ma moved them all into Old Colony (by then the two oldest boys had enlisted) and Flynn and her ma started putting on the weight that the father lost. By the time we were in high school, Flynn and her ma were identical: round as playground balls with skinny, pink legs.

My dad was the opposite of Flynn's, tall and loud and handsome, and used to the attention he got when he walked into a room. He grew up in Southie, and everyone in the Town knew him from when he ran track for Southie High. He had massive, shapely legs, which he liked to show off, and from May to October he wore Bermuda shorts so you could watch the muscles in his thighs shift below the madras plaid. His senior year he went All-State for hurdles and high jump and then All-American, and he got his picture in the *Herald*'s Sunday sports section. He said he fell for Ma because she had a fresh mouth— not swears, she didn't swear then either—but she was sharp, and he liked that, plus the orange hair, which was prettier then, and she had a great figure, which meant skinny with big boobs. Ma said Dad was a peacock, used to turning heads.

She paid no attention to him at first. She went out with Frank Flanagan whose father owned two stores in the Town, and who played football, which was more exciting than track. He wasn't quarterback or anything flashy; he played center, which meant he bent over and snapped the ball back and never made a touchdown, but still he got the smart uniform with the pads and the helmet, and he didn't have to play in his Skivvies, Ma said.

Ma and Dad didn't go out until after high school. Ma never graduated, she got pregnant instead. Frank Flanagan said he was one of maybe five guys who could have been the father, which Ma said was what Adam told Eve when she got pregnant in the Garden of Eden. Ma went to stay with her sister, Helen, in the suburbs, and she had Hap out there, at Carney Hospital, where her brother-in-law worked. Ma and Dad didn't meet again until Hap was about two months old, and Ma was pushing him in his baby carriage out by Castle Island, and Dad went running by. There weren't too many unmarried girls who kept their babies in 1956 in South Boston, and Ma scandalized everyone by not being ashamed and by walking the baby in broad daylight and naming him Happy besides. And by flirting with my father. Dad said he married Ma because she was open-minded and her own person—she didn't care what people thought. A woman ahead of her time, he said. Ma says what they love you for in the beginning is what they leave you for in the end.

They had me right away and, for all intents and purposes, my dad was Hap's dad too. While I was growing up, he drove a truck for Shaughnessy the Mover; the fleet was docked in Southie, out by the old Navy Yard, and he and Ma got along pretty well until she got pregnant with Timmy. This was six years after the twins. We didn't live in Old Harbor then. We lived in a triple-decker in the East End, not the fanciest part, but we had the whole first floor to ourselves plus the yard. Plus, we were in walking distance to Gate of Heaven, which I loved. That church was practically a cathedral.

Ma and Dad fought the whole time she was pregnant. He kept saying he'd thought she was using something; they couldn't afford another kid; he'd have to take a second job, which was guaranteed to kill him. She said of course she was using something; she was the only practicing Catholic in South Boston who was. If Father Keenan found out, he'd refuse her communion, and she couldn't bear to let anything come between her and communion, not even her own sins.

Dad started coming home very late from work, singing. You'd think singing was the kind of thing that would always be nice, always make you feel better, especially since he had a beautiful voice, prettier than Ma's; people were forever asking him to sing at wakes and christenings and so forth, which he loved to do, but his singing late at night was not uplifting. Hap and me would pretend to be asleep when he opened the door to our room to check on us. Usually he'd stand and sing, his hands gripping the door frame above his handsome head, his long, muscular arms suspended; but sometimes he just stood there, and we could hear him breathing and, in either case, I tried to make my own breath regular and slow.

Once, he stayed out the whole night, and the next morning Ma wouldn't let him in the front door. She'd figured he'd show up the following day all penitent, but he called from Chicago a week later and said he couldn't raise another man's son.

I remember the call. Ma stood with her back to me in the front hall, curled around the phone. She argued every fight the same—her voice, her body bending toward you. She said, loudly, into the phone: "What does that have to do with anything, you've been raising Hap for ten years?"

I remember the pause. Then Dad must have said, something like, *I'm not talking about Hap.* Because Ma said, Fuck you, which was the one and only time I ever heard her swear.

We moved into the Old Harbor Projects after that, and Ma never forgave Dad for making her take a step down. I met Flynn the week that Dad left. She was bouncing a basketball on the playground at Gate of Heaven. Most girls couldn't even reach the basket in fourth grade, their arms were too weak, but Flynn could dribble and shoot.

"Wanna play?" she asked, after I'd been watching her.

We played Twenty-One, only we only got up to 6–2 when the bell rang. "I won," Flynn said, "unless you want to keep playing the same game tomorrow."

She bounced the ball as we walked across the playground to get in line. One of the new, younger nuns, Sister Gail, called out to us; we were supposed to hold all balls after the bell rang; we were supposed to be silent. I could hear the other girls' shoes scrape against the asphalt as they ran to get in line. I could hear the ping! ping! of the bouncing leather ball.

Sister Gail put her hands around her mouth to make a megaphone. "Patty Flynn!" Like the other young nuns, she wore regular, drab clothes and a short black veil instead of a habit.

Flynn said, "You're the kid that lights the fires, right?"

I nodded. I was watching the ball leave her fingers. She could almost dribble without looking down.

"Wanna know something?" She took a step and tried to bounce the ball between her legs. "My dad's a bookie." The ball veered off one of her knees and rolled away.

I shrugged. "So."

She took two giant steps and captured the ball again. "Do you even know what that means?"

I nodded.

"No way you know." She propped the ball against her hip.

"He takes bets."

Flynn had dark brown hair then, and it fell, unwashed, around her face. She pushed a stringy strand behind one ear. "He's going to jail."

"Patricia. Flynn." Sister Gail waved her arms in the air. She was young, but she was no pushover.

I said, "When?"

"After Thanksgiving."

"He should wait until after Christmas."

She started dribbling again. "*They* should wait for after Christmas," she corrected. "It's not like he has any choice."

"My dad left," I said, and started to cry.

"Don't be a sap," Flynn said. "Don't cry." And she tossed me the basketball.

7

I'D LIKE TO TELL YOU THAT SOMETHING HAPPENED between Elly and me during *On the Waterfront*. Something serious. I'd like to tell you that when Flynn got up to go to the concession stand for more popcorn, I put my hand on top of Elly's hand on top of my thigh, that I turned to kiss her on the mouth. I'd like to tell you that, because she was a college girl and more experienced; Elly frenched me back and then undid the top button of her black blouse.

But I've already decided to tell the truth about the first year of the busing, and that isn't what happened. To begin with, Flynn did not go back to the concession stand. So when I crossed my left leg over my right leg to hide Elly's hand from view, my movement drew Flynn's gaze instead of blocking it, and there was Elly's hand between my thighs, and Flynn frowned. Then she grimaced and made a noise, and we stared at each other. Flynn got up from her seat, and her big bucket of popcorn spilled to the floor.

I stood up and said, "No, you stay. I'll go."

She made another noise and we just stood there. She looked like a giant bumblebee in her puffy, black and yellow Bruins jacket.

A man in the row behind us said, "Down in front."

I said, "Pardon me," and leaned across Elly and bent to pick up Flynn's popcorn. I handed Flynn the mostly empty bucket, my face red from the bending and from embarrassment and from the wave of heat I felt, like an oven door opening, from where Elly was sitting.

Flynn frowned at the bucket. She said, softly, "What the fuck, Ann?" But it was more to herself than to me.

The man behind us said, "I'm calling the manager if you don't sit down."

I straightened up and said "Pardon me" again and looked past Elly to the complaining man. It was the Black with the Jesus beard, the one who'd banged on Flynn's window, and I realized there'd be no pleasing him—some Blacks are just like that, impatient—and now there'd be no pleasing Flynn, maybe never again.

But then Elly said, "Wait. Patricia."

She was sitting between us, tilted nervously forward, sort of folded over her knees, her arms wrapped around her shins. Splotches of red showed through her white powder. I wanted to tell her that no one I knew, no one in the world, called Flynn, *Patricia*.

Elly said, "I can explain." Then she sat back and completely let go of her shins. Now there was considerably more of her considerable cleavage to look at.

And I knew without raising my eyes that Flynn was watching me look, watching me stare. It was an awful moment, my eyes fixed on the clean, curving line between Elly's powdery boobs; I actually had to close my eyes to stop myself from staring. Then Flynn grunted and my skin gushed red and I knew there was no way to pretend I didn't see what I was seeing, didn't feel what I was feeling. I turned and hurried out of the movie theater.

I hurried through the lobby, out past the empty ticket

booth, and before long I was running. I ran three and a half blocks down Huntington Avenue, toward the nearest T stop, which was Symphony. It had started to rain. I ran past dozens of lazy Northeastern students who looked at me like I was a freak, like, Hey, man, what's the rush? And I wanted to scream: Stop staring, you're the freaks, for Christ's sake, in your stupid hippie clothes and your dumb tie-dyed T-shirts. It's the seventies, I wanted to shout! The sixties are over, you assholes, you missed it, don't you realize?

But I didn't do that. I just ran down the stairs at the Symphony stop and bought a token and paced back and forth on the platform, sweating but cold from the winter rain, waiting for the train. It came, one of those lurching underground trolley cars with an accordion middle that bends around corners, and I got on; it wasn't even crowded. I was too agitated to sit, so I stood holding a shiny silver pole by one of the doors. There was a lump in my throat, and I wanted to cry, but couldn't.

I gripped the pole as the trolley staggered forward. Inside my jean jacket, I could feel the letters to Mademoiselle Eugénie. If only I'd thrown them away, like a normal person. If only I hadn't burned them.

The trolley car jerked to a stop and more people got on and off. I decided to sit. I crossed my legs and stared at the place on my thigh where Elly had put her hand. To tell the truth, I never would have guessed about Elly. Never ever. Right then, I pictured Marlon Brando, his striped pajamas, his dark, muscular hands on the white throat of Vivien Leigh, and a wave of heat rippled across my thighs, across the seat of my pants. I blushed, ashamed to be so turned on.

I stood up. Tried to shake the feeling out of my legs and bum. Could any of these people tell? I realized they could be having their own weird trips, and I wouldn't know. Flynn had an eye for males, for the way their pants hung, but I never did. There was a hippie couple reading the paper together, the woman leaning over the man's shoulder, her long blond braid dangling between her boobs. She wasn't wearing a bra. There were two Blacks in the car. An old lady wearing a long purple parka over her dress and sturdy black shoes that laced up. She sat reading the Bible in one of the seats reserved for old people. I stared at the few inches of skin that showed between the edge of her parka and the tops of her shoes. The other Black was a girl about my age with a medium-sized Afro and a boxy leather jacket that couldn't have been warm enough; she sat looking out the window even though we were underground and there was nothing to see. I had the strange sensation (I'd had it before) of seeing people's bodies as separate from them.

At Park Street, I got off to switch to the outbound red line. The red line serves both South Boston and Dorchester. Dorchester used to be all Irish. Now it's Irish east of Washington Street, heading toward Southie, and Black west of Washington, heading toward Roxbury. Roxbury used to be all Irish too. Everything, it seems, used to be all Irish at one time or another in the city of Boston. The orange line goes into Roxbury. It's an elevated train. I've never ridden the orange line.

When my train came, the doors opened and a million people got off, and a million more got on, including the Black girl in the boxy jacket, but I just stood there. People shoved me going past, and a guy in a wool cap asked what my freaking problem was. When the doors closed for good, I turned around and went back to the green line. I got on another accordion trolley car, this one headed in a different direction, inbound. I told myself that I had no idea where I was going.

Usually, when I saw people's bodies as separate from them, the main thing I noticed was how vulnerable they were. How risky it was to just walk around. To eat and drink and go to the bathroom. As if any need at all left us way too exposed.

It may surprise you to know that I had sex with a guy once. Flynn's middle brother, Danny. This was right before he left for

Vietnam. He had finished the year of basic training and was counting the days before shipping out. Come on, he'd said, I might get killed in Vietnam. Also he said: I like the tomboy thing. Most guys don't but I do. Besides, he said, I'll tell everyone I got your cherry.

Danny was twenty, but he always hung out with younger kids. He was immature, everyone agreed, but I kind of liked him, he had a good sense of humor. He had thick black eyebrows that came together above his nose in a single startling line. Otherwise, his face was boyish. When he smiled, he only opened his mouth on one side. His teeth were crooked. Come on, he said, I'll tell everyone you're not a lezzie. I'll tell Hap.

He wore me down. We were out by the old Navy Yard, driving around. He was teaching me how to drive a stick shift. He said the car belonged to a friend of a friend, which meant that it was stolen, but not by him. I thought, why not, I might as well try it, what have I got to lose? I thought, maybe, for a couple of months, I won't have to fight my way home from school. And maybe Hap would leave me alone. I closed my eyes and pictured a girl on Carson Beach. To tell the truth, I didn't mind it. I mean, once he got going, I liked the feeling of Danny inside me. It was the getting there that was not so pleasant. He thought my boobs were too small; he didn't say it, but when he lifted my sweatshirt, his funny half-smile sort of fell, and I could see he was disappointed. Still, he kept tweaking them and tweaking them—his fingers felt dry—until I had to say, Danny, give me a break, they don't come off. Afterward, we were both so embarrassed, we didn't tell anyone.

8

Sometimes, when you do something daring, something that will change the rest of your life, you have to coach yourself, you have to tell yourself, step by step, what it is you are doing. You have to go over it and over it so as not to lose heart. For instance, when I tongued Laura Miskinis in the stairwell by the metal shop in ninth grade, I had to tell myself over and over that the experience would be worth whatever came after. And it was, the feeling of being inside her. It was worth it. What came after was that the metal shop teacher knocked me down. How long does that last?

Other times, when you do something life changing, you have to pretend not to notice, you have to pretend not to understand what it is that you're doing. When Dr. McGraugh was trying to get me to stop lighting fires, he said the consequences of what I was doing were bigger, more serious, more grave than the gestures I was making. More grave—one of his favorite expressions—than the pleasure, the impulse, of match to paper.

In order to do what came next, I had to pretend I did not understand the consequences of my actions. Maybe it would be better to say, I had to refuse to imagine them. Refuse to think. Instead of thinking, I told myself that I couldn't go home. Couldn't open the door to our apartment until Ma was asleep in her bed, unconscious, dead to the sounds of her children, if not to the world.

I rode the green line to Brookline, then a bus to Jamaica Plain. I remembered just enough from my previous visit to find Mademoiselle Eugénie's house, the drab brown triple-decker with the cream trim. I stood across the street in the shadow of a scrawny tree. By now, it was dark out, and the icy rain had turned to snow.

I stomped my feet to keep warm. It may sound silly—strange—but on the bus, I had pictured Mademoiselle Eugénie opening the front door, inviting me inside. *Bonjour, Ann*, she had said, *Bonjour!* Now standing there, I realized that something was wrong: Every light on every floor was turned on. Light poured out the windows onto the sidewalk, onto the pathetic mailbox and beyond.

For a second, I stared at the mailbox. More than anything, I wished I was the kind of person who would have sent those letters already. I wished I was. I hurried across the street. Inside my jacket pocket, only half the letters were intact. I brought them to my nose, my mouth; smelled the vanished smoke. My tongue reached out and touched the curling edges. Burned paper tasted clean, appealing, the ash sticking to the back of my throat. I stuffed the letters inside the mailbox and watched several black flakes swirl to the ground. When I got back across the street, that triple-decker looked like a lighthouse flashing alarm.

I stayed there for quite a while, watching the snow fall. The white flakes looked fat and wet and heavy. My breath made clouds. I tried to imagine Mademoiselle Eugénie opening the letters, but all I could picture was Flynn, her disgusted frown. I stomped my feet and buttoned up all the buttons of my jean jacket. I wished I'd had a scarf or a hat, anything.

Nothing happened, no one came, no one even passed by. In the other houses, the living room windows glowed ghostly blue. Probably, everyone was inside, watching TV. Probably, everyone was cozy, comfortable: at home. Mademoiselle Eugénie's house was too bright, too still. I noticed then—how long did it take me?—her front door was open. Not wide, just a foot or so, like she'd left in a hurry, too anxious to worry about pulling the door closed behind her. It seemed danger-ous, a house open like that, exposed; it made *me* anxious, so I ran back across the street and up the three, crumbly steps. But instead of simply shutting the door, like I'd planned, I stepped inside.

It was like nothing I'd ever done before—honest to God—and my heart was pumping loud. For some kids in the Town, breaking into houses was practically a specialty, but not for me. I stood still and listened to the wild sound. To my left was a set of stairs. I was standing in Mademoiselle Eugénie's front hall! I couldn't believe it. I felt giddy, elated. Also, petrified. Even though I was pretty certain the place was empty, I called out, *Hello, Hello!* I listened to my voice bounce from room to room.

After a minute, my heart began to slow. Underneath the stairs was a square table piled high with winter hats and scarves and gloves, and underneath the table, a row of rubber boots. Mademoiselle Eugénie did not live by herself. I picked up one of the scarves and wrapped it around my neck. It was incredi-bly soft, plum-colored, made of wool, but not scratchy; that scarf would never give you a rash. I put on a hat, a French beret; they were wicked popular. Did it belong to Mademoiselle Eugénie, or to one of her friends? Did everyone wear French berets in Paris, France? I glanced in the mirror above the square table. *Bonjour! Bonjour!*

The harsh light made the empty house seem even quieter, as if everything was caught, frozen in the brightness. I started up the stairs, which were worn-out, creaky. The sound exploded into the silent house. I had seen that in the movies—the creaking steps. Almost everyone I knew lived in apartments, mostly one floor. Actually, everyone I knew lived in the *same* apartment, more or less: the projects. The problem with the movies was they made you think you had more experience than you actually did.

I rested my hand on the banister. *Her* banister. Her hallway. Living room. The living room was like the outside of the house, temporary-feeling. A dingy yellow couch was propped up by phone books on one side. Catty-corner to the couch, an old-fashioned, round television stood on its own legs. Across from the sofa was a reclined Barcalounger and two tired-looking beanbag chairs, a red and a pink. I tried the Barcalounger first, but it wouldn't close, wouldn't sit up like a regular chair. Then I lowered myself onto the deflated pink beanbag. It was not what you would call comfortable. My knees came up past my chin.

On my right was a fireplace with a mantel. On the mantel were two pictures—framed photographs—of Blacks: an unsmiling woman in a white graduation cap, a long-legged kid in short shorts holding a basketball. Was it a boy, a girl? Staring at those pictures, I realized this was a Black house. Which surprised me. I mean, I didn't think of Mademoiselle Eugénie as Black like that. She was different, her own person. So *individual*. I'm not sure who I had imagined her living with; probably I had not imagined anyone, had not pictured anyone at all.

Perhaps it goes without saying, but I'd never been in a Black house before. It made me anxious, agitated. I looked around. Full of dread. Everything was different now. Black sofa and chairs, Black Barcalounger. Like a veil had been lifted: Black television with Black rabbit ears. I had the urge to go back downstairs and start over again. Black banister and Black hallway, Black scarves and boots. Now the dinginess had a particular quality. I tasted ash again at the back of my throat.

I struggled up, out of the beanbag chair. I shook my head. You might think, at that point, I would want to get out of there. But some, well, curiosity held me where I was. Last summer, Hap got arrested twice for breaking into houses on the Point (breaking and entering was not his specialty either). Both times, the houses were empty, the rich people away on vacation. Both times, he'd just squatted there, inside, until some worker—the gardener or handyman—showed up and called the police. When the cops asked him what he was doing in the rich people's houses, Hap had said he was just trying it out. He meant: the good life. That's not what this was. Of course, I wanted to know about Mademoiselle Eugénie, the way she lived. But this was different.

The Black hallway ran the length of the house. Beyond the living room, were two doors. I figured, maybe, the Black bedrooms. I crept along. I felt inexplicably sad. In ninth grade, when I got in trouble for tonguing Laura Miskinis in the ear, the headmaster had called me a pervert. I knew then, he had the wrong word. Perverse means twisted. What I'd done was simple, straightforward: a tongue, an ear, a current of feeling. What I was doing now, in Mademoiselle Eugénie's house, was perverse. Sneaking around. A lone White in a Black house. Trespassing.

I opened the first door. The room was big, with two windows overlooking the street. Right away, I smelled her smell; I recognized it from school. I don't mean perfume. I stepped inside, closed the door. For a minute, I stood still, catching my breath. My heart was pounding against my chest. What on earth would I say if someone discovered me there?

Last summer, when the cops arrived, they told Hap he was stupid, a jerk, just waiting around to get caught. In the squad car, on the way to the police station, he said they'd laughed and laughed. Now I wondered if Hap had felt what I did. Stepping inside that house, her room, was scary, sure, but it was also, well, exhilarating. I knew it was against the law, and knowing that made me feel uninhibited, free. In that way, it was similar to setting fires.

I went around the bedroom, touching her things; I couldn't help it. She didn't have much. A single bed pushed against the wall, at its foot, a red-plaid blanket, the edges trimmed in satin. At the head of the bed was a cardboard dresser—we had the same kind at home. This one was painted blue, no knick-knacks, no trinkets, no corny figurines. Opposite the bed stood a solitary chair and reading lamp, a stack of books. I sat in the upholstered chair. It felt stiff, uncomfortable. Most of the books were in French. *La damné de la terre,* the top one said. Usually I could guess someone's personality from the stuff they kept, but that room was sparse. Maybe—what did I know?—maybe you didn't bring knickknacks all the way from Paris, France. One of the books, *L'Étranger,* she'd given us in school.

Just beyond the dresser was the closet. Inside, all the clothes faced the same direction. Mademoiselle Eugénie wore strange, tight, French clothes, everything belted. One dress was mustard green with gold rectangles; another had orange-and-white stripes that ran along the diagonal. A third was purple. I fingered the gaudy material. Six pairs of shoes lined up like soldiers under the dresses. They had fat heels. I guessed more of her personality showed here, inside the closet. I shut the door.

At the front of the room, between the two windows, was a small wooden desk, a child's desk, with a matching chair. On top of the desk were letters and envelopes and so forth. I knew I shouldn't have, but I sat down in the tiny chair and looked at the letters.

The paper was thin, practically see-through, light blue instead of white. She had funny handwriting—French handwriting (even their penmanship was different!)—I couldn't make out the words. *Chère maman,* maybe one of them said. I tried to picture her mother. Probably, she would be the exact same color. I realized, if I'd sent my letters, and Mademoiselle Eugénie had written back, this is where she would have sat. *Chère Ann,* she would have wrote. For a second, I pictured her there, curved back, dark head tilted toward the see-through paper. It made me mad; honestly, it made me hate myself for being a coward. Once, in school, we'd had a genuine conversation, just the two of us. I felt suddenly cold, as if a gust of wind—except no windows were open—and I shivered; only Mademoiselle Eugénie has a better word for it: *frissonner.* I tucked my hands up into my armpits to get warm.

Beneath the letter to her mother was a picture postcard of a Black man wearing the exact same French beret as me. Even though the hats were wicked popular, it seemed like a strange coincidence. I picked up the postcard. The man looked familiar. Where had I seen him before? He sat in a giant wicker chair with a round back, like a cobra's hood, looming above him. The chair was like a throne. In one hand, the man held a rifle; in the other hand, unbelievably, he held a spear. A white rug with zebra stripes, maybe an actual animal skin, was placed at his feet. It was some kind of joke—I didn't get it—*spear chucker*—I got that much—*har, har, har*—but why have your picture taken?—it made no sense to me. *Bush boogies back to Africa* was what the kids always chanted at school.

The picture gave me a funny feeling. What on earth was it doing here? Mademoiselle Eugénie was not like that. She was not angry. She did not blame you for being White. She did not blame you, period. Which was why she was so nice to be around. On the back of the postcard was a sentence stamped in red ink. The block letters were raggedy, incomplete, but I was able to make them out: PROPERTY OF THE BLACK PANTHER PARTY, it said.

I remembered who the man was.

I felt in my pocket for matches.

PART TWO

That Night
in Jamaica Plain

9

After my first session with Dr. McGraugh, he invited Ma to join us. His office was in one of the rich houses on the Point, and he sat with his back to a row of windows that looked out onto Boston Bay. Because there was so much light coming in through the windows, his face looked dark, almost severe. I thought probably he'd been athletic once. I could feel Ma notice him—the bones in her spine—when she stepped into the room.

Before she even sat, Dr. McGraugh started talking about how pyromaniacs didn't set fire to things because they were angry or antisocial. He said they set fire to things for pleasure. For the experience of gratification. For release. I could hear his own crisp pleasure in saying these unexpected things. I wasn't a true pyromaniac, he told her, because I was so pissed off.

At the time, I remember ducking my head, hiding my smile. I remember thinking: How stupid was Dr. McGraugh? As if anger could be separated from pleasure.

My one genuine conversation with Mademoiselle Eugénie took place on Halloween. I know the actual date because that day a Southie kid came to school in a ghost costume—his mother's nasty old sheet with two eyes cut out. At lunch, in the cafeteria, someone taped a sign to his back that read: "Keep the spooks out of South Boston." Table after table of Southie kids burst out laughing when they saw the sign, which drew the attention of the Blacks, who sat together at lunch. In the end, the kid in the sheet got stabbed. Everyone who was there said it was amazing how fast the sheet went from white to red.

Right away, the school emptied out. All the Whites went home. The Blacks couldn't leave the building; they had to wait for the buses, which wouldn't come until the end of the day. They were stranded. Half the Town showed up outside and surrounded the school. When the fight in the cafeteria broke out, I was in Mademoiselle Eugénie's class. We were doing a unit on geography. A giant color map of the world hung from the ceiling. The map was in French. *Mappemonde,* it said. She stood next to it and pointed to different countries and had us repeat the names.

La France.

La Belgique.

Le Portugal.

She was wearing a short purple dress with yellow piping along the collar and edges, plus these fat yellow buttons down the center. On anyone else it would have looked outmoded. She pointed out the countries enthusiastically, sometimes ducking behind the map to reach the other side.

Le Québec.

L'Algérie.

La Martinique.

She asked us to come up and point to the countries where the people spoke French. No one raised their hand. No one even looked at her. As a rule, people didn't look her in the eye. During the first week of school, Mademoiselle Eugénie had used the giant pull-down map to show us Senegal, where her family was from. The kids in class had licked their lips and looked at each other in disbelief. They shook their heads. Who on earth would admit that?

"*Bon.*" Mademoiselle Eugénie glanced around the room. "*Peut-être,* you would like to travel one day? Where would you like to visit? *Quel pays?*"

Again, no response.

She put her hands on her hips, but not in a challenging way. Her arms were long and thin and she wore silver bracelets on her left wrist. We stared at her black Black skin. The bracelets jangled at her hip. "You want to spend your whole lives then, *aux États-Unis?*"

A girl in the back raised her hand. "My brother's been to Vietnam."

A round of snickers.

"*Ah, oui. Le Vietnam.*" I couldn't tell if she hadn't heard them, or, maybe, didn't understand what the snickers meant. "*Très bien, Catherine.*" She hurried to the other side of the map. Maybe she understood, but didn't care.

Vietnam was tiny, rose-colored. It had the same name in French as in English. Mademoiselle Eugénie pointed with a long finger. "*Le Vietnam* was a colony of *la France, avant la guerre.*"

A few kids picked up their heads.

"*Vous comprenez,* before the war?"

Right then, a Southie kid threw open the door. "Fucking nigger stabbed Paulie Fahey." No one moved. Behind him was a wave of noise. We sat stiff in our chairs as the sound rolled up the hall and overtook him, overtook our room. We could hear other classrooms, beyond our own, emptying out.

Mademoiselle Eugénie brought a hand to the back of her head. She smoothed her shiny hair. I wondered if they used the same word in France. Or did they say something else? She frowned, looking around the room. The frown was thoughtful, not mad. She seemed more perplexed than afraid. "*Le Viet-*

nam was a colony of *la France* in the same fashion as *le Séné-gal. Vous comprenez?"*

The Whites got up and left. The Blacks waited for the Whites to go, then left together, as a group. I couldn't move, couldn't take my eyes off Mademoiselle Eugénie. She wrapped her arms around herself. She pursed her lips and said, *"Bon,"* which was a kind of verbal tic. It meant, "good," which obviously things weren't. She went over to the window and parted the blinds and looked out. Her long neck made me think of the swan boats in the public garden.

She said something to herself, under her breath, but I didn't catch it.

I said, "What's the word in French for swan?"

She looked up, irritated, and said, *"Comment?"*

I blushed, shaking my head. "Forget it. Never mind."

She went back to peering between the blinds. We could hear the police sirens and radios, the voices of the demonstrators gathering.

I had ridden on the swan boats once, when I was little and my father hadn't left yet and Hap and me still got along. The whole family had had to stand in line for an hour, and I remembered the Jell-O tiredness in my knees and wanting to ask my dad to carry me, but I was too big for that, four maybe, and when we finally got on the boat, I realized the giant swans weren't real birds; their long, stiff necks were wooden; their sad, elegant faces were painted and would always stay that way. It was unsettling to me even then, a face that wouldn't change; the swans made me nervous, their big black eyes refusing to blink. Now I said, "A friend of mine's in Vietnam."

She let go of the blind. *"Vraiment?"*

I nodded.

She came and sat at the student desk in front of mine. *"Depuis longtemps?"* Her face was open again, full of concern. I shrugged. "A year."

"But the war is over, *non*?"

"He's just keeping the peace."

"*Ah, oui.*" She nodded. She was so close, I could feel her breath on my face. She studied her hands, the pink palms. She played with the jangling bracelets on her wrist.

I said, "What does that mean, Vietnam and Senegal were colonies of France?"

She nodded, pleased at the question. "It means *les Français* were in charge, running the government. The United States was a colony of *l'Angleterre,* yes?"

"A long time ago."

"*Bon. Le Vietnam* was a French colony. *Récemment. Le Sénégal* also."

I was confused. I thought of colonial times, the Revolutionary War, the Boston Tea Party. In Boston every year, there were reenactments. They threw tea in the harbor, charged up Bunker Hill. I said, "Danny enlisted because the brochure said that in the Navy you got to travel all over the world."

"Do you worry about him, *ton ami*?"

I shrugged. "Not really."

She looked surprised.

"Danny can take care of himself. Besides, I'm thinking of enlisting. Girls can join the navy too. And I want to travel."

She sat back. She started to speak, then stopped.

"I mean, I don't want to spend the rest of my life here. In South Boston."

She nodded. "*C'est très bien, les voyages. Très instructif, vous comprenez?* Very educational. And where would you go, what countries would you visit?"

"France."

She smiled. "*C'est vrai?*"

I nodded, blushing.

"Where else?"

"Ireland."

"*L'Irlande, en Français.*"

"*L'Irlande.*"

"*Bon.*"

"That's where my family's from."

"*Ah, oui?*"

"Can't you tell? Most people can tell."

She shook her head.

"They say I have a face like the map of Ireland."

"*Comment?*"

"A face like the map of Ireland. It's an expression. It means I look Irish—the red hair and freckles. You can tell where I'm from just by looking at my face."

"*Ah, oui,* an idiom." She stood and went over to the map.

"Everyone has red hair in my family."

"*Vraiment?*" She drew a line with her finger from France to Ireland. Ireland was brown on the map, not green, which was usually how you saw it. She traced its outline, then looked back and forth from me to the map. She smiled, her finger moving slowly along the edges. "I like that, yes. The face of the map of *l'Irlande. Très bien.*" She nodded. "And would you say—?" She hesitated. She tapped France on the map. It was blue. "*C'est moi, là?* The map *de la France?*"

Of course, I didn't know what to say to that. But before I could embarrass myself, she tipped her head back and laughed. The sound was full and clear like a bell. Expansive. I'd never heard her laugh. It seemed to me that everything she did—I mean ordinary things—had a kind of grace. I felt a surge of joy inside my chest. I laughed back.

She stopped and looked at me, and I caught myself. But then she said it again: "*C'est moi, le visage de la France!*" And we laughed together, her mouth opening wide. We laughed until we heard a terrible crash from outside. We went over to the windows. At one end of G Street, several hundred yards from the school, a police car was tipped on its side. A kid from the

SBLA—you could see the green armband—was standing on the tipped-over car, waving a huge American flag. Hundreds of people were cheering. The kid was ecstatic; he stomped his feet on the police car. At one point, he almost lost his balance, the heavy flag pitching him forward. The crowd applauded when he righted himself. I knew that I knew him—but couldn't produce the name. I turned away, rested my backside against the glass. Probably, I was the only White student still inside the building. Probably I was. "I think, maybe, I'd better be going."

"*Oui, oui, bien sûr.*"

"I mean, I bet it's not smart for me to be here."

"*Bon, bon.*" She nodded vigorously.

"I mean, for either of us."

She seemed embarrassed.

When I got to the door, I turned around. I said, "What are you going to do?"

She glanced at the empty classroom. She shrugged and her painted eyebrows fluttered on her forehead. She was more beautiful than any of us. More beautiful than my whole country. I said, blurted out, really: "Your class is my favorite class all day."

"*Ah, bon?*"

"You teach us words in French that I didn't know their meaning in English. *Abandonnement. Rectifier.* Relinquish."

"*Très bien, Ann.*"

"*Nostalgie.*"

"Ah, this word, you must take care. It is not the exact same as the English. It means homesickness."

I nodded. "I think I have *nostalgie* for South Boston before the busing."

She pursed her lips, looked back toward the windows. The demonstrators were getting louder. For a minute, we listened to the voice of someone on a megaphone trying to calm the crowd. The voice was shrill, distorted.

I was afraid that I had offended her. "Is it like this in Paris? I mean, do you fight like we do here?"

"*Non.*"

"So you all get along?"

"*Non.*"

"Do you—are you homesick, then?"

She turned back to me. She smiled with just the corners of her mouth. "I find that home is never *exactement* how we remember it."

"I guess not."

"The word for swan is *cygne*."

"Pardon me?"

She shrugged. "You asked me the word *en Français* for swan."

My face went red.

"What made you think of the swans?"

"Nothing. I don't know. I think I have to be going now."

"*Bien sûr.*"

And so, like that, cringing, stupid, I left.

10

I was still sitting at Mademoiselle Eugénie's desk, staring at the photo of the Black man, fingering the matches in my pocket, when the police arrived. Two cars. No sirens, no flashing lights, but I heard them and looked up. My heart went through the roof. It was the one thing Ma asked for: no more calls from the police.

A cop opened the back door of the first cruiser, and Mademoiselle Eugénie stepped out. Carefully, one foot at a time. She bent the stiff stalk of her neck. I knew then that something had happened to her, that they had not come to arrest me. She moved like she was practicing how to walk. Still, I panicked. I threw myself onto the floor, half crawling, half running to the top of the stairs. If I made it down, before they got inside, perhaps I could run out the back. I heard more car doors opening, then slamming shut. I heard the sound of someone's footsteps running toward the house.

In my panic, I slipped on the second step, my ankle buckling. I didn't fall, but sort of slid down several stairs at once. I caught myself halfway and took the remaining steps upright, but I'd twisted my ankle. It didn't matter much because by then the front door was open and two cops plus Mademoiselle

Eugénie were standing inside. She looked beyond sad, beyond devastated. The cops held their hands out to her, kind of ushering, but didn't touch her, a weird halo of police hands. Her posture was not American. For a second, we all just stood there, me on one foot, surprised.

One of the cops—he had a round, pushed-in face and a crew cut, his white hair like the bristles of a brush—said, "And who's this, another roommate?" This last word got a peculiar emphasis.

Mademoiselle Eugénie didn't answer him. Now her face was expressionless, blank. She asked me a question in French. She actually used my name, but I didn't know what the question meant. I shrugged, embarrassed. Her voice was flat. The cops were staring at me. How I wished I'd paid better attention in class! We could have had a private conversation in French, right there, in front of the police. I felt this terror rising in my throat, so I reached down and touched my twisted ankle and said, "I think, maybe, I broke my foot."

It was not the worst strategy. It bought me time, maybe a minute or two. The police moved us both farther inside, down the hallway past the staircase, toward the back of the house. One of them gave me his arm to lean on so that I could hop, and the whole time I was hopping, I was thinking, What's my story, what the fuck's my story? Behind us, the front door opened and more cops and Mademoiselle Eugénie's actual roommates came inside.

The kitchen ran the width of the house, its cabinets, stove, and fridge all pressed against one wall. A long red table stood opposite the cabinets. The white-haired cop sat me and Mademoiselle Eugénie down. I smelled bacon grease and cigarettes, ammonia. The cabinets were painted the same cheerful color as the table. Of all the rooms of the house, this one felt the most lived-in. On the table was a napkin holder made from popsicle sticks and a clump of plastic flowers. The second cop knelt to check my ankle; he was a big man with big hands, but his touch was surprisingly gentle. I rubbed my eyes and made phony ouching sounds as he felt for the bones in my feet.

When I looked up, I saw that I'd never been in a room with so many Blacks before. I started to count the number of Black faces—it's a habit of mine since the busing—but then I recognized Devonne and Rochelle, the two Blacks from my basketball team. I couldn't believe it! They stood with their backs to the kitchen counter, their arms folded across their chests. They glanced from me to Mademoiselle Eugénie then back to me, their dark faces fuming. Somehow they had made her acquaintance! What on earth were they doing here? It was beyond strange. Beyond coincidence. To tell the truth, it made me furious—*why in God's name?*—but then Rochelle, the tall one, must have had had the exact same thought, because she lifted her chin in my direction and said: "What's *she* doing here?"

The cop with the caved-in face interrupted. "You mean, she doesn't live here?"

Rochelle shook her head. "Uh-uh. Name's Ann Ahern. She's from Southie. She's on our basketball team."

Rochelle kept looking at Mademoiselle Eugénie. We all did. She was sitting incredibly still, her straight back impossibly straight, her delicate, dark head bent. She stared at her hands in her lap as if she was praying, but I didn't think she was. Rochelle glanced in my direction. "Nice hat," she said.

I reached up. The French beret! The purple scarf! I yanked them off.

The cop said, "So, let me get this straight? She's a friend of yours from *South Boston*?"

Rochelle shook her head. "That's no friend of mine." Her face was long and thin; if she were White, she would have looked horsey. Instead, she looked sad.

Devonne grunted. "Never passes us the ball. I mean *never*."

I wanted to say, It's *you* who don't pass *me* the ball! But of course I didn't. Couldn't.

"Old Ball Hog never speaks to us either." Devonne's close braids gave her a kind of blunt expression. "Ask her if she knows our names. I have never, not once, even heard her whisper our names."

The cop who was checking my foot stood. He ducked his head awkwardly, as if the ceiling was low, which it wasn't. "It's not broken, Sergeant. She should get it looked at, but it's definitely not broken."

"If she's not a friend of yours," the sergeant said carefully, "what's she doing here?"

The cops looked at me. Just inside the doorway were two older females, a Black and a White. Behind them, another pair of White cops, these barrel-chested, squat. The older females stared at Mademoiselle Eugénie.

"Are you a member of the SBLA?"

I shook my head.

Rochelle turned to the sergeant. "Her best friend's in ROAR."

Devonne snorted. "Every single one of them's in ROAR."

The sergeant said, "How'd you get that shiner there?"

I reached up and touched my cheek.

Rochelle said, "Your fat friend, she's a regular Louise Day Hicks."

I wanted to respond, to stand up for Flynn.

"How'd you get inside?" That was the older Black female. She was acorn brown. She stepped farther into the room.

I opened my mouth, but no sound came out. I cleared my throat, once, twice. Finally, I said: "It was open."

"So you just came in?" She moved closer to the table.

I nodded.

Her hair fell in tight braids to her chin, sort of Prince Valiant. She tilted her head, and the shells on the ends of the braids swung together, gently clacking. "Just like that?"

"Yes."

"Who are you, Goldilocks?"

Har, har, har. Everyone laughed at that: the cops, the Blacks, even the White roommate.

"I sure don't want to think about who that makes us."

More laughter. Her voice was deep, like a man's. Attention-grabbing. Instinctively, I reached down and rubbed my ankle.

Devonne sucked her teeth. "I'll show her broken. If she wants to know about broken."

Mademoiselle Eugénie raised her head. Her eyes were huge, sunken. "Ann, she is a student of mine. I have been asking her to come here, to deliver some books."

I couldn't believe it.

Neither could anyone else. The cops exchanged looks. Devonne made that tsk-ing sound again and Rochelle frowned. The Black female in the Prince Valiant braids went over to Mademoiselle Eugénie. She had an air of being in charge; even the cops were watching everything she did. She knelt down, put an arm around the back of Mademoiselle Eugénie's chair. Very gently, she said, "Jean?"

Mademoiselle Eugénie touched the long stem of her neck, nodded. Then she said it again, this time more forcefully. "I have been asking Ann to come here to deliver some books."

I tried to keep the astonishment out of my face. I coughed, still trying to clear my throat. "I put the books where you said. Upstairs, next to your reading chair."

Mademoiselle Eugénie eyeballed me. She looked beyond tired, beyond worn; whatever had happened had drained the brightness from her face. The lush intensity. But if she was surprised by what I had said, she didn't show it. "*Bon,*" she said, nodding. "*Bon.*"

11

I LEFT MY *CARTABLE* AT SCHOOL. HOW DO YOU SAY . . . the bag for the school books? Inside were the examinations of the students. I am driving, when suddenly I cannot—put, put, poom—I stop. The car has no more of the petrol. At first, I do not know what to do. At first, I am just sitting there. But then I remember the petrol station who is just over the next hill. You see, it is the same route that I take every day to the school."

We were upstairs, in the living room, Mademoiselle Eugénie on the slanted yellow couch. The police had left. They'd lost interest in me, but not in her. Tomorrow she had to report to the nearest precinct house and make a statement, what the sergeant had called a deposition.

Mademoiselle Eugénie sat sidesaddle, her spindly legs tucked beneath her. Devonne and Rochelle had collapsed on the beanbag chairs, and the older females were perched protectively on the arms of the yellow sofa. I sat on the floor, as far away from the beanbag chairs as I could position myself without leaving the room.

Mademoiselle Eugénie had insisted I stay. I did not know why. It was late, she'd said, almost midnight; if I left now, it would not be safe. But that was the excuse, not the reason, we all knew that. She even offered to call my mother, to tell her where I was, but I said no. Ma would kill me for staying out all night, *snap your spine*, was what she said. But just the thought of telling her where I was—well—I couldn't quite finish the thought.

To tell the truth, I was confused about what had happened between me and Mademoiselle Eugénie, what transpired. I mean, why had she lied on my behalf? Why had she saved me from the police? Of course, I was incredibly pleased, incredibly relieved. We were on the same side. But which side was that, exactly? I had to ask myself—was it possible?—if Mademoiselle Eugénie had feelings for me. Just thinking that thought, I felt this revving inside, like an engine that wouldn't stop, like a conveyor belt I couldn't get on or off. It was thrilling sure, but it was also, I didn't know, unsettling. Did she feel the revving too? I mean, I knew I was just some stupid kid, but stranger things had happened, hadn't they? (In English class, they hammered us again and again with *Romeo and Juliet,* the Montagues and Capulets.) That time, when we'd spoken in school, Mademoiselle Eugénie had tipped back her head and laughed, and I'd seen all her teeth. I knew then it was a kind of gift. The shared laugh, but also, the open mouth: the pink roof and the beautiful, straight, white teeth.

For the second time, she said, "How do you say . . . the bag for the school books?"

The older Black female—Rochelle's aunt, it turned out, her name was Colleen Washington—said, quietly, "We say book bag, just as you did. Or, maybe, rucksack."

Mademoiselle Eugénie nodded and repeated the word *rucksack.* Her voice was musical, but not frivolous, not light.

The aunt said, "Jean, were you afraid? Driving through Southie?"

Mademoiselle Eugénie puckered her mouth thoughtfully. She nodded. "At first, with all the *manifestations,* I have Ruth drive with me." She glanced at the White female. "But I have stopped doing that now, it is almost a month."

I closed my eyes. From where I was sitting on the floor, I could picture her mouth. The robin's egg.

"I take the petrol can from the trunk of the automobile. A bright red can with a long, er, what do you call it? A long nose? After a little half hour, maybe less, I return to the automobile and there are *trois garçons,* three boys, sitting inside."

"Did you recognize them?"

A long pause.

I opened my eyes.

Rochelle's aunt slipped off the arm of the sofa onto the yellow cushion. "Jean, can you identify the boys?"

Mademoiselle Eugénie raised her shoulders up, in a delicate shrug, and for the first time, I realized how bony they were.

"Perhaps from school? From the demonstrations in the neighborhood?"

Mademoiselle Eugénie brought a hand to her face and rubbed her eyes. Suddenly I got this panicky feeling that I knew those boys. And that somehow, she knew that I did. Was that why she'd lied to the police on my behalf? Was she expecting something back? Some kind of exchange? The thought made me queasy, sick. Probably, she didn't have feelings for me at all. Probably not. Finally, Mademoiselle Eugénie sighed, shaking her head. She dropped her hand and looked at Colleen Washington. "I am not certain. They are familiar yes, but I do not know for certain."

The aunt nodded. "What happened next?"

"I ask what it is that they are doing in the automobile. But they do not answer. I think to myself, they have how many years? Seventeen, eighteen? Then I see: They are staring at the petrol can. I step back from the automobile, but it is too late. One of the *garçons* he is already next to me. I do not see him exiting the automobile, but *le voilà,* his elbow touching mine. He is tall, *maigre.* I notice then, the band, the green band around his arm. They are all wearing it."

I felt a sharp pain in my throat. My brother had joined the SBLA because he had nothing else to do, no job, and Ma wouldn't let him enlist. Mostly Hap liked harassing the police.

"The boys, they do not speak to each other. Their eyes only are moving. It is as if the sound of their voice will make them stop. The one who took the can, now he is shaking it over the car. He could be, how do you say, watering the nature? The plants? The petrol is spilling everywhere. He jumps back: He is not wanting the petrol on his clothes. He laughs—it is the noise of a dog barking—he cannot stop. The others watch, their hands in the pocket of their jean."

Out the corner of my eye, I could see Devonne and Rochelle hunched forward on the beanbag chairs. I thought of the many fires I'd built as a kid. At Gate of Heaven. On Carson Beach. Out by Ponkapoag Lake, once, with my Milton cousins. In the alleyways and Dumpsters of Old Harbor. I thought of the fire I had set that morning in the bathroom of my mother's house. I felt nauseated. Self-disgusted.

"When she burns, the car, at first there are many flames. But when the petrol is gone she looks—how do you say?—the opposite of *spectacle.* The Volkswagen, she is small, but she seems to fall in, not out—*plus petite, plus petite,* like a snail." Mademoiselle Eugénie scrunched her elegant body in imitation of the shrinking car. "The smoke, it is so thick, the car, she disappears. I am choking on the dirty smoke. The boys have tied a napkin around their mouth. I think that they are looking like cowboys. *C'est impossible,* I am saying to myself. It is the wild west of America! The boys want very much for me to watch. One of them, the tall one with the petrol can, he is touching my arm. He is holding me still. I feel the heat of the flame against my face. '*Regarde, regarde,*' he says. Look, look!"

For a minute, no one spoke. I was sure the others were staring at me, as if the fire was all my fault, as if I had had something to do with it. But when I raised my eyes, I saw that they
were looking at her, at Mademoiselle Eugénie, her velvet face.
She was weeping.

What on earth was wrong with me! Here Mademoiselle
Eugénie had just told this terrible story, and I was worried
about myself! About what the others thought! I was in love
with her and, yet, here I was, unsympathetic, holding myself
apart. The truth was, all I kept thinking about was whether I
knew those boys. Or rather, how well I did.

Colleen Washington edged closer to Mademoiselle Eugénie.
She took one of her hands and patted it. The aunt was gentle,
she was being kind; but at the same time, you could see her
single-mindedness. "The leader—the one who poured the
gasoline—you said he was tall?"

Mademoiselle Eugénie nodded.

"What else do you remember?"

Mademoiselle Eugénie sighed. She was tired. She took her
hand back from the aunt and wiped her wet face, first one side,
then the other. "The hair, it is red. On the skin—how do you
say, the spots on the skin?"

I thought, Don't let it be Hap.

"The eyes are blue."

I couldn't bear it.

She raised her head and looked at me. Her painted-on eyebrows were gone. "What is the word, *Ann*?"

I felt the color drain from my face. "What is . . . what word?"

"For the spots, on the skin? You were mentioning it before?
It is a long time ago."

"Freckles?" My voice was small.

"*Ah, oui.* Freckles. *C'est ça.*" She nodded.

I looked away. We were thinking the exact same thought. I
was sure of it. To tell the truth, I had to get out of there. I just

couldn't bear the sound of her musical voice pronouncing those words. I looked at the stairs. How fast could I run? I reached down, touched my ankle; it was hardly even sore.

If only I could have had my feelings separate, one at a time. Perhaps then. But no, they had to come all at once. Honestly, I wanted to kill those boys. Whoever they were: Hap or one of his stupid friends, I didn't care. What had happened to Mademoiselle Eugénie was beyond awful. Beyond words. I wanted to kill those boys with my bare hands. And I wanted to protect her. But at the same time, I didn't want to be a Benedict Arnold. I *couldn't* be. It just wasn't in me. I thought of Flynn, my family. I hated them for making me see Mademoiselle Eugénie the way that they did. For making me place her, so to speak, geographically. I'd always thought of her as different, unique. Outside of what was happening. An oasis of pleasure. Honest to God, I had to get out of there. It would be better for everyone. It made me feel intensely ashamed, but probably Mademoiselle Eugénie would be better off without me there. Probably she would.

Then she said, "I am thinking—*peut-être*—that I saw *le garçon* once before." Her voice was soft, quiet. She faced the aunt. "How did you call him, the leader? Once before. At *la manifestation.* He was—perhaps—he was the boy carrying *le drapeau*?" Now her eyes were on my hands, my face; without turning her head, she was looking at me. "Do you remember, *Ann*? The boy with the flag."

To tell the truth, I had always thought I was an adventurous person. I had always thought, given the chance, I'd be the first one to leave South Boston. Now I wanted to go back. To be home in bed, safe. Not to be feeling what I was feeling then. In grade school, at Gate of Heaven, Sister Gail had taught us about Joan of Arc. How'd she'd saved France from the Protestants. How she'd worn men's clothes, ridden horses into battle. It was embarrassing to admit, but I'd always thought, given the chance, I'd be like that. Heroic. That was the trouble with being a girl: You never knew because you never got the chance. Now here it was, and I wanted to run. Bolt. I started to cough. I coughed and coughed. The others looked over. I actually started to choke. My face went red. I stood up. I was choking on how much I hated myself. I raised my arms up, over my head. I remembered that in basketball, you could play injured—you could run up and down the court on a twisted knee or ankle—if you told yourself it didn't hurt. If you held the idea of yourself, uninjured, carefully in your head. So I did that.

I told myself that I was Joan of Arc, that I was saving myself from the Protestants. I held this idea in my head: I was not a coward. Just the opposite. I was saving myself to fight another day. I pictured myself with short hair, carrying the flag of France. I looked like a woman who looked like a man. By then, I had stopped coughing and everyone, everyone was staring at me.

Mademoiselle Eugénie said, *"Qu'est-ce qui se passe, Ann?"*

Which was when I ran for the stairs. Black stairs. I thundered down. Black table with Black hats and boots. For less than a second, I saw myself in the Black mirror over the table. I almost burst into tears. I looked wild-eyed, scared. My red hair flying about my face. I was not who I thought I was. I was not. I shouted, crazy, into the mirror, *"Bonjour! Bonjour!"* For the first time, I wondered what on earth she was doing here. Mademoiselle Eugénie. What was she doing in my country?

PART THREE

Map of Ireland

12

On the bus to Springfield, to the Basketball Hall of Fame, Coach Curry sat next to Devonne and Rochelle. When we traveled to games, he always took the seat in front of theirs—his body turned sideways so he could see the back, as well as the front, of the bus—because none of us would sit near them. I myself sat three seats away, and across the aisle, my head and arms resting on the dark green seat back in front of me. Instead of closing my eyes, which I pretended to do, I peeked underneath my armpit. Coach Curry drew a diagram in the palm of his hand. Devonne and Rochelle watched blankly.

The coach was taking us to the Hall of Fame to see some corny exhibit about the history of professional basketball, and how wonderful it was, they'd never been segregated, no Negro Leagues, like in professional baseball, and how everybody, Black and White, always got along, yadda, yadda. He wanted us to see the exhibit because so far this season our team had lost every game due to the refusal of Blacks to pass to Whites and vice versa. In other words, Devonne passed only to Rochelle; Rochelle passed only to Devonne; and us Whites passed only to one another.

It was the first week in January and the light was almost gone from the sky by the time we saw the first green sign that said Springfield. The bus was quiet except for the rattling noise the engine made. No one but Coach Curry wanted to see that corny exhibit anyway. I stopped spying on Rochelle and Devonne and put my head against the window, something we weren't ever allowed to do on bus rides in the city. The glass was cold, and I pressed my cheek against it to absorb the chill. I sighed, but it was a fake sigh—fake boredom, fake exasperation. I was grateful to be on the bus, grateful to be going somewhere different.

Since that night in Jamaica Plain, at Mademoiselle Eugénie's house, I'd been grounded, stuck at home except for basketball games and practice. Ma had been waiting up for me, and when I fell through the door—maybe 4 A.M.; I'd had to run-walk the whole way home—right away I could see she'd grown old from the waiting. Her face looked stiff. A muscle in her jaw stood out, taut, like a piece of wax string. I felt bad, but I still refused to tell her where I'd been, and she'd yelled, saying she'd snap my spine if I ended up pregnant before graduating Southie High. I was so surprised by her line of thought, and so exhausted from the night I'd had, and so, I didn't know, amazed by the distance between those two things, that I laughed out loud. We were sitting at the kitchen table, and I knew the laugh was wrong, but I couldn't help myself, it was like a reflex, and she jumped up and raised her hand to slap me. I leaned so far back in my chair that it fell over. We stayed like that for a couple of seconds, and I said, Go ahead, because I half wanted her to kick me with her pointy shoe (so I could hate her even more than I already did), but she refused.

The Hall of Fame was a long, low, sandy-brick building, with lots of windows facing the street, like the wing of a Holiday Inn. It was part of Springfield College, which itself was pretty bland, all the buildings square and new, nothing inspiring, or impressively old like at Northeastern.

Coach Curry made us walk single file from the bus to the entrance, and I could hear in his voice the anxiety teachers get whenever they're off school grounds. We stood inside the lobby while our coach talked to the man in charge of school groups. Devonne and Rochelle leaned against the cinder-block wall opposite the ticket window, talking soft. Above them were posters advertising the exhibits on display. One said, FAMOUS HOOP RIVALRIES: BILL RUSSELL VERSUS WILT THE STILT. Two tall Blacks were reaching up, their long arms and armpits, even their hips, pressing against each other. I heard the word, "ignorant," and glanced back at the girls. They were arguing. Devonne counted something out on her fingers, offering them, insistent, to Rochelle. Rochelle kept shaking her head, No.

I'd never seen them argue. It gave me a funny feeling, I did not know why. We hadn't spoken since that night at Mademoiselle Eugénie's house. Not at practice, not in the hallways.

It may sound strange, but it was a relief to me that we didn't speak. I wanted to forget that night in Jamaica Plain; I wanted to forget everything I saw and felt, the sensation of being in a Black house. Even more than that, I wanted to forget what had happened to Mademoiselle Eugénie, and how she thought I knew something about it. At school, there were way too many reminders.

For one, Mademoiselle Eugénie did not return right away. The headmaster announced that she was under a doctor's care and could not come back until he approved. Meanwhile, an actual police investigation was under way—the fire had made the papers—there was pressure from Blacks to find the White perpetrators—and actual detectives visited the school in hopes of identifying those boys. The fact that she stayed away made her look peculiar, almost guilty in some strange way. But of what? I overheard the headmaster say that her absence was disconcerting, a word I'd had to look up: It means disturbing. Or embarrassing. Either way I missed her. I missed seeing her in the hallways. She was always a surprise there, always bright and dark at once. Vivid, I guess you might say, at a time when everyone else was trying to blend in, trying their hardest not to stand out, myself included. So life at school ended up being easier without her.

The cops interviewed all the kids in the SBLA and half the kids in ROAR. Of course, they interviewed me about my night in Jamaica Plain. Ma missed work to be there—they can't interview minors without the parent present—and she sat smoking while I answered their questions in the headmaster's dinky office. I remember the detectives stood so close that I had to crane my neck to make eye contact. Ma was in the chair next to mine, and I could feel her obnoxious smile whenever I told the detectives something I'd refused to tell her. But Ma's triumph was not long-lived, not well thought out. The more she heard about where I'd been, the more anxious and confused she got. When it was over and we stood to go, she kept opening and closing her mouth. She didn't say anything the whole way home. Later, word got around school that I'd spent the night in a Black house. Which was disconcerting to my classmates.

Now in the lobby of the Hall of Fame, I watched Rochelle fold her arms over her chest and grimace. Her long face looked suddenly longer. Ma always said that some people were old souls. Rochelle's face had this weariness, which was more than being tired. Devonne pivoted away from her and slammed inside the double glass doors of the Hall of Fame. Coach Curry glanced up from his conversation. The other Whites, our two forwards, stood like they did at practice, hands in their pockets, poking with their sneakers at the lobby floor, pretending not to notice what was happening.

Inside, the Hall of Fame looked more like a high school

than a college. We watched Devonne stalk up and down the main hall, her sneakers squeaking on the linoleum floor. Off this hallway was a series of classrooms that held the exhibits. Coach Curry dragged Devonne into the first room, the rest of us trailing. A giant placard gave the history of the Hall of Fame, which was in Springfield because the inventor had taught there. Next to the placard, in a square glass case, was the original peach basket. Coach Curry made us crowd around. He kept one hand on Devonne's shoulder. Rochelle stood on the opposite side of the display, which was as far apart as I'd ever seen the two of them stand. With his free hand, Coach took out his glasses and read about the first basketball game. Devonne's arms hung by her sides; they were like two of mine, straining the seams of her parka. She hated White people, you could tell just from the way she stood.

Against every wall in the room were glass cases filled with old-time pictures and ancient uniforms and even a pair of some old player's worn-out sneakers. I closed my eyes and listened to Coach Curry's voice drone on and on. There was something depressing about the Hall of Fame; don't get me wrong, I'm a basketball fan, I truly am, but there was something small about it. Confining. I thought of fish tanks in an aquarium, the lonely lobsters trapped inside, forever separated from the blue crab. I didn't think Rochelle hated Whites the same as Devonne; I could not say why. I raised my hand and got permission to go to the bathroom.

It was a relief to leave the others behind; I didn't have to pee, I was just taking some air, taking a break from Coach Curry's exhausting optimism. I poked my head into all the exhibit rooms. The first one had pictures of old-time teams that traveled around before the actual NBA. I stood in front of a photo of the Boston Eagles, the men carefully posed, one guy stretched on the floor, holding the ball, which showed the year, 1928, in white letters. The expression on his face was faraway, dreamy. The other players were arranged around him, all of them touching: a hand on a knee, an arm on a shoulder, their faces rigid (for the camera, I thought), but not their bodies. It was surprising to see the White men draped like that, touching, and I couldn't help but wonder whether anyone else had noticed. Also in the case, set to one side of the photograph, was the original 1928 ball. It was brown leather, smooth instead of pebbly, with stitched white seams. It looked shrunken. Even I could palm a ball that small.

In the next room was the advertised exhibit about the two Black rivals. All the pictures were blown-up, life-sized. Of course I'd heard of Wilt Chamberlain and Bill Russell. My dad had been a Celtics fan, and once he took Hap and me to a game. I remember because I wet my pants—I'd told Dad I had to go, but he kept saying, Just one more minute, just one more minute. My cold legs chafed on the walk home. Bill Russell was a Boston Celtic then. He was unbelievably tall and thin. At the game, Dad's favorite player, a guard named Bob Cousy, retired. When they lifted Cousy's uniform up, into the rafters, Bill Russell hugged him. Dad said that Russell was an ugly son of gun, but could he play.

I was looking at one of the giant photos of Russell—the men's shorts seemed shorter then—plus he was all legs—I could see where the muscle attached to the bone—when Coach Curry came in and grabbed me by the arm. "I said no wandering off." Bill Russell's eyes were flat, black, not dreamy. Coach's thumb pressed that soft spot inside the elbow, and I winced as he yanked me into the hallway. "This is a team activity. A team sport."

He's not big, Coach Curry. He was a guard himself, just under six foot, and he's still pretty fit, plus he's got this boyish quality like there's way too much energy under his skin. I hated to disappoint him, which I pretty much always did. He steered me through a set of doors, out past the exhibit rooms, and into a small auditorium where the rest of the team stood, letting their eyes adjust to the dark. On a pull-down screen up front was a slide show about the history of the NBA. My eyes followed the column of light to the rickety projector in back. Except for us, the auditorium was empty. A man's recorded voice said something about the very first NBA finals. I listened to the familiar slicing sound the slide projector made. On the screen was a picture of a group of skinny men, Black and White, running awkwardly down the court.

Like an usher at church, Coach Curry led us down the center aisle, motioning for us to sit. Devonne stomped to the end of the row and took the last seat. Then Rochelle sat pointedly not-next to her. That is, she left an empty seat between them. Which was when it occurred to me, for the first time, that they were girlfriends.

They were *girlfriends*!

Suddenly, it was obvious—why had it taken me so long? I felt a wave of embarrassment, first for not knowing, then for figuring it out. An image of naked Black females flashed in my mind, and all the blood rushed to my face. It seemed something too private to know. Then I remembered the funny feeling I'd had when I'd seen Devonne and Rochelle arguing, and I realized I'd felt exposed.

Now Coach was hissing at me to take a seat, I was holding up the line, and so I stumbled forward, dropping into the seat next to the empty seat next to Rochelle. The White forwards followed suit, and so our team sat spread out like that, taking up maximum space, like guys on the T, and I could hear Coach Curry sigh when he sat down at the end of our row. This was not what he'd had in mind, not his vision of brotherly basketball love, and I felt bad for the coach, I truly did, but there was nothing he could do: You can't force people to change their minds.

In profile, Rochelle's Afro was huge, like a satellite moon, but her head seemed small, no pronounced jaw or chin; in the dark theater her dark skin shone kind of buttery. First Elly, and now these two! I never in a million years would have thought. Rochelle was looking straight at the screen. I wondered if Mademoiselle Eugénie knew, or if the aunt did; then I wondered, if they *did* know, what they thought.

Once, my sophomore year, I went downtown to this bar that I'd heard about from Danny Flynn. I stood across the street for an hour or so and watched the women go in and out. Danny Flynn had said that with two women, one was always the man. I had no idea about that. Right then, like she could read my mind, Rochelle turned and looked at me. I didn't think my skin could get any more red, but it did. I brought my hand to my neck and felt the flush of color there. Rochelle watched my hand at my throat. Then she raised her eyebrows in this pointed way, and I knew she was asking me a question, but all I could do was shake my head, like, Leave me alone. Like, I don't know what you're asking. But of course I did. I knew what she was asking. Instead of answering, I turned back to the screen, to the awkwardly running men.

13

THE NEXT DAY, DURING OUR GAME AGAINST EAST BOSTON
High, Rochelle threw a ball at my head. You could say it was a
pass, except that she threw the ball exceptionally hard, when I
wasn't looking. We were only a few feet apart, and the ball hit
the side of my head, just above my temple. The impact was so
great, I fell down. Coach Curry called for a medical time-out.
We were losing to East Boston High 15–4.

Perhaps it goes without saying that in basketball you're *supposed* to pass when your teammates aren't looking, but you're
also supposed to *know* they're just *pretending* not to look,
they've got you out the corner of their eye, out their peripheral
vision, etc. Great players are said to have great peripheral
vision. Pretending not to look is a strategy to fool the other
team, but when Rochelle threw the ball at my head, I wasn't
pretending anything. The ref blew her whistle, and Coach
Curry hurried over and crouched beside me and wouldn't let
me stand until he'd made sure I wasn't hurt. He asked me who
the President of the United States was. He held up two fingers
and made me follow them with my eyes. More so, even, than
the fall, Coach Curry's attentions were humiliating.

My next possession, first thing, I threw the ball at Rochelle.

I threw it as hard as I could with both hands. I swear I wanted to kill her. But Rochelle was already at half-court, her back to me; she was heading in her lazy, nonchalant way toward the basket. At the last second, she turned around and caught the ball. It was not what I had intended. She went in for a layup and scored. Without meaning to, I'd thrown her a pass! When she landed back on the ground, she looked over at me and smiled. Like I didn't know what irony was! That smile enraged me. I tried to hit her with the ball again and again. Each time, she caught it and scored. At halftime, the game was close, 18–15. Rochelle had scored every one of our points, except for a layup she'd dropped back to Devonne.

In the locker room, Coach Curry passed out fresh-cut orange sections and Dixie cups with water and talked excitedly about offensive domination. "You just have to *choose* to win," he said, looking first at me, then Rochelle.

"Just choose to win." Before he finished his speech, I pushed Rochelle, face-first, against the lockers. The metallic sound echoed through the other, empty stalls. When she turned around, she looked more surprised than anything.

Rochelle was maybe four inches taller than me. Plus she had that high, billowy Afro. I must have looked crazy standing there, hands raised, waiting for a fight. Then Devonne elbowed me, hard, between the shoulder blades. I hadn't even seen her move in my direction. I fell forward, one arm out to catch myself—you always picture the lungs in the chest, at the front of the rib cage, but really, they're in the back, the back—and Rochelle stepped easily out of my way. The jab knocked the wind out of me. Coach Curry shouted at Devonne, at the rest of the girls, but what I remember most is the feel of the locker grill against my face, and how slowly the time seemed to pass without my breathing, and, finally, that pinpoint in my lungs that pricked itself open and let some air in. I remember the taste of the warm air. Part salt, part orange section. Still collapsed forward, I closed my eyes and pictured those little sacs that do your breathing—like clumps of grapes—we'd studied them in biology: *alveoli.*

We beat East Boston 32–24. Coach Curry benched Devonne and me, but it didn't matter. For the rest of the game, the White forwards, plus two girls who hardly ever played, benchwarmers, also White, passed the ball to Rochelle.

14

THE ONLY THING I'D EVER SUCCESSFULLY BURNED DOWN was a phone booth. A lot of paper—garbage—had been left inside. Garbage up to my thigh. I was thirteen, the last year in junior high; this was when the state told Ma that I had to visit Dr. McGraugh or they'd take me away from her.

The phone booth was near the water, on the sidewalk that ran alongside Carson Beach. It was always out of order. *Always.* The tongue you put the receiver on was broken. I didn't think anyone would miss that useless phone. But the police came by and saw the smoke and flames.

I was sitting yards away, on the pebbly sand, watching the paper burn. There must have been something else inside—turpentine or a hair spray bottle—something to keep it going, because it went. It went for a long time, the flames shooting straight up and licking at the glass sides, the glass door, like they were trapped inside, trying to get out, which, of course, they were.

I'd just learned that Sister Gail was leaving town. She'd been ordered by her order to someplace hot and far, like New Mexico or Alabama, I could not remember. We'd stayed in touch since I'd left Gate of Heaven; now she coached CYO basketball. After practice we'd sit at the back of the church and talk. It was always so cool and quiet. She wore CYO sweatpants and a sweatshirt, plus the short veil. She had pimples, but was not allowed to wear makeup to cover them up. For a while I actually thought about becoming a nun, although I'd never told anyone, not even Sister Gail. What appealed to me was the peace and quiet. Also, the way people saw you as set apart, but not in a way that enraged them.

That morning, when she told me she had to leave Southie, I asked her what it meant to have a calling, and she said it was like getting an invitation to something which, after you accepted it, defined you, made you somehow different than you were before it came. The word she used was *designation*. As she spoke, she made the sign of the cross against my forehead with her thumb. I liked the idea of being changed like that, suddenly, from the outside.

I said, "Don't you, you know, miss guys?"

She shook her head. "Not particularly."

"My problem is, I don't believe in God." Then I told her: no flicker, no flame. Her whole face sort of expanded, but in a mournful way, and she touched me again, this time pressing the heel of her palm against my forehead and letting her long fingers rest on top of my head. Her lips moved, and I could see she was praying, so I closed my eyes, and I felt something then, but I was pretty sure it was not what she had intended.

Eventually, the city knocked the burned phone booth down, then the rest along Carson Beach because the mothers in the projects complained that the booths were used for selling drugs, which was stupid, because they were used for selling drugs, but so was everywhere else: people's apartments, the courtyards, the intersections along Old Colony; the phone booths had no monopoly. In the end, the only evidence of what I'd done were the black streaks on the sidewalk.

As part of my penance for my night in Jamaica Plain, Ma

made me take my baby brother to the library every Saturday. I held Timmy's hand as we crossed Prebble, then Old Colony, tracing the rotary that separated the two projects across from Carson Beach. It was unusually warm out for February, the snow melting under our sneakers. Ma had given us change for the bus, but I wanted to walk. I squeezed Timmy's hand, which was sweaty in an earnest, little-kid way.

I usually liked hanging out with my baby brother. Most people in my family were high-strung, like Ma, but Timmy had this relaxed quality. He was very low key. Plus he had zero expectations. I thought that came from being the youngest, from being disappointed so many times by so many people in so many different ways. But today, I wanted to be by myself. I kept thinking about Rochelle hitting me on the head with the basketball. I kept wondering, What was her intention—to humiliate me? Or to get the team passing? Once, Dr. McGraugh had said that sometimes, when bad things happened, it was because people *wanted* them to, even if they didn't realize it. He was trying to get me to say that I was setting fires because I wanted to get caught.

With his free hand, Timmy clutched a brown paper bag filled with library books he was going to return. I kept pulling him along. We passed Flynn's family's apartment, which was right on the corner, 1190 Columbia Road, and for less than a second I thought about stopping in, something I'd done maybe a thousand times before. The Old Colony Project was made of square, flat-topped buildings three stories high. Even though they were three floors, they seemed short, squat, close to the ground. Between the brick buildings were archways that led to interior courtyards. I never went through one of those archways without Flynn. For the most part, the kids from Old Colony didn't mix with kids from Old Harbor, which was considered a slightly better project (meaning less poor). The distance between the two was only a few hundred yards, but that didn't matter, they were separate universes with separate cliques. Except that Flynn and me always did mix. We always did.

Timmy paused and switched the paper bag to his other hand. He'd been reading since kindergarten, which was years ahead of anyone else in my family. Ma said he was so smart he would probably go to college on a full scholarship. I looked down and saw he was working hard to keep up: two or three steps for every one of mine. But he didn't complain, just watched his own feet, concentrating. He wore his strawberry hair in a Southie cut, which meant parted severe, straight down the middle, and blown back at the sides. (Most mornings the twins blew it dry for him.) He had a freckled, Opie face and ears that stood out, just the littlest bit, from his head. I hurried us along Columbia Road. I wanted to stop at Dorchester Heights before going to the library.

The Heights was a silly old Revolutionary War monument, but it was my favorite place in all of South Boston because it was so high up. You could see the rest of the city from Dorchester Heights, and I liked going up there to sort things out. In my neighborhood, solitude was hard to come by. Dr. McGraugh had said one way to understand someone's intention was to look at the consequences of their action. Right then, I wanted to climb to the Heights and examine the consequences of Rochelle's throwing a ball at my head.

As we walked, the air pressed wet and soft against my skin. Here it was winter, but you could still smell the salt off the water, which was the thing I liked best about my neighborhood: the proximity. You'd think people from the projects would spend half their lives on Carson Beach, what they called the Irish Riviera, escaping the summer heat, escaping the asphalt jungle, etc. But not many people from Old Harbor or Old Colony went. Instead, they sunbathed on the project roofs or in little plastic wading pools in their courtyards. They never crossed the lanes of traffic between the projects and the water. Ma said that was the village mentality.

Timmy tugged on my arm. "Can you slow down? The library's not going anywhere."

"Sorry," I said, and got that funny feeling you get when your baby brother talks like an adult. "I want you to see something first."

"You're holding my hand too tight."

"Sorry. Sorry."

Ma herself did not have the village mentality; she was from City Point, not the projects; her father had been a longshoreman who worked extra shifts his whole life to keep his family out of public housing. She loved anything that took her away from Old Harbor, especially Carson Beach, which she said was excellent for a city beach: The MDC still sent trucks to sift the sand, and it was only a little bit rocky, with actual seashells and seaweed, in addition to the trash you'd expect, cigarette butts, empty cartons, and crushed cans of beer and tonic. Lots of rubbers. Ma always took us swimming when the tide was going out, so the garbage in the water—cardboard boxes and strange, large, unrecognizable pieces of Styrofoam—streamed out into Boston Bay.

Timmy stopped walking and put down his paper bag full of books and wrung out his tired hands.

"Hey," I said. "That bag will get wet."

"Here, you carry it."

"What have you got in here?" The top book on the pile was a Dr. Seuss, a favorite of mine. "*Would you, could you, in a box?*"

Timmy rolled his eyes. "That's for babies."

"So how's school this year?"

Timmy scratched one of his jug ears. He never talked about what it was like getting bused to Roxbury.

The wet bottom of the brown paper bag ripped in my

hands. I held it up. "Hey, I thought you were supposed to be the genius in the family."

He squinted up at me, smiling. "But now look who's carrying all the books."

I swatted at his carefully parted hair and he ducked. On Thomas, we climbed the concrete stairs that led to the smallish hill, at one time a bona fide park, which was Dorchester Heights. It looked better in winter; the snow covered the grassless grounds and hid the trash that people left behind. A lot of people liked to walk their dogs up there, and this old man told me once that the acid in the dogs' pee was what kept the grass from growing. The actual monument part looked like the top of a Protestant church, a steeple, mounted on marble, with a corny inscription about some pathetic old Revolutionary War soldiers. The marble base was covered with graffiti.

Timmy said, "I don't know why you like it up here. It's so dirty."

"Don't you like seeing the rest of the city?"

He shrugged.

"Come on."

At the base of the monument Timmy stood and read the inscription out loud. I turned and looked out. The Heights didn't get tourists, like the Old North Church; it was not a big draw, like Paul Revere, but I loved the view. You could see the water on both sides, Carson Beach and the inner harbor, plus downtown, and the expressways north and south; you could see Back Bay and the Public Garden, Beacon Hill; you could probably even see Roxbury, although I was never able to find it. I looked for the Blue Hills, off in the distance, the suburbs where my cousins lived. I looked for Jamaica Plain, for Mademoiselle Eugénie's house. She still had not returned to school. The longer she stayed away, the worse the rumors got. Probably that doctor who had to approve her coming back was a shrink, like Dr. McGraugh.

Timmy kept reading the inscription out loud; it said something about building a fort in one night; it said something about arduous effort. I thought the main consequence of Rochelle's throwing the ball at my head was humiliation. She'd humiliated me. But also, she'd singled me out. I felt that. She'd singled me out by humiliating me. What did that mean? When Timmy finished reading the inscription, he said, "What did you want to show me?"

"Just this. The view."

He looked out. "So?"

"Don't say that."

He wrinkled his freckled nose.

"Don't say, 'So.' I hate it when you say, 'So.'"

Above us, some seagulls screeched. The sky was gray, but had streaks of cream in it—a spring sky in the middle of winter. I pointed toward East Boston. "Look, that plane's getting ready to land at Logan."

"So?"

I glanced at my brother.

"So. So. So."

I had the urge to slap him. Instead, I said, "Maybe we can find Roxbury. If we look hard enough, maybe we can even find your school."

"I hate it there."

"Come on, you love school."

He shook his head vigorously. "Not anymore."

"Don't say that."

He sighed.

The weak February sun bounced off the melting snow, making everything brighter. The brightness made my eyes ache. I said, "Listen. Never mind what I just said. Tell me about school. Tell me anything you want."

He hesitated. He glanced over his shoulder and lowered his voice. "Hap says—he says you're a white nigger."

I was surprised. "Do you even know what that means?"

He started nodding, but then stopped himself. "Not really." He shrugged. "Hap says the SBLA is going to chase all the white niggers out of Southie."

My eyes throbbed. I hated the idea that Hap was having conversations with Timmy. "You shouldn't talk like that. Ma doesn't like it."

He looked down, dragged his toe in the snow.

"Besides, Hap doesn't know what he's talking about."

Under the snow was a bottle cap; Timmy kicked at it with his wet sneaker.

I said, "Are you, you know, worried about that? That I'll have to leave Southie?"

Timmy looked up. "I can't go to the bathroom."

"What?"

"At school. The Black kids run the bathrooms."

"What Black kids?"

"Sixth graders. They beat you up. Take your money."

"They beat up the little kids?"

He nodded.

"Do you want me to come?"

He shook his head.

"Do you want me to beat the crap out of those sixth graders?"

He kept shaking his head. "That will only make it worse." He started walking down the hill. He looked like a little old man, talking to himself. "There's nothing you can do. Nothing."

And I got this pain in my throat because I knew he was right.

15

AFTER THE GAME AGAINST EAST BOSTON, ROCHELLE and me started to become—what? Not exactly friends, but not exactly enemies. I don't mean that we hung out or even spoke. We didn't. We watched each other. On the court, but also, off. We watched each other without seeming to. We could follow each other out the corner of our eye, out our peripheral vision, and no one knew.

What the feeling was? I couldn't say. Maybe it wasn't a feeling, maybe it was just a thought: I *see* you. *I see you seeing me.* Plus, our team had started winning. We beat Charlestown and Revere. Hyde Park. There was an article in the *South Boston Tribune* about how Coach Curry had turned the girls' team around. And just when we seemed to have established a rhythm, Devonne quit the team. Everyone, everyone was surprised.

Coach Curry tried to talk her out of it. His classroom was next to the gym—he taught Health and Hygiene when he wasn't coaching—and we could hear him pleading with her when we passed by that day on the way to practice. Except we didn't pass by, we (the White players) stood on tiptoe in front of his wooden door, trying to see through the tiny rectangle of glass, which was too high up. No matter what he said, she wouldn't budge, or tell him why, and his voice climbed higher and higher.

I wondered, Did she quit because Rochelle had started the team passing? Or because the two of them had broken up? I wasn't certain about the latter, although the signs were there; for one thing, they *weren't* always together in the hallways. And when they were together, they didn't talk much, didn't look each other in the eye. At practice, I watched Rochelle's face for signs of sadness, but she was in the habit of showing us nothing, no smile or frown, no trace of feeling.

When our team played Dorchester, I started at point. I couldn't believe it! After all those years playing second fiddle to Flynn! Dorchester is half Black, but their team was 100 percent, and when we walked in the gym, I thought, We're going to get creamed. But we didn't. I kept passing the ball. Rochelle scored twenty-one points. I swear she was more like a guard than a center; she liked to score; she liked having possession of the ball. I'd have bet, when she played with boys, she played guard. Like I said, the two of us never said a word, but before the first jump ball, the whole team standing on the court, she squatted down to tie her sneaker right in front of me.

"Their guard has this tick." Her voice was matter-of-fact, informational. "Dribbles right, then left, then she goes up to her right. I'm talking every single shot. My girl's weak on the left. You can pick her off when she switches to her left."

Which I did. Maybe eight or nine times. And each time I stole the ball, I'd look up and there was Rochelle, waiting for the pass, already underneath the basket.

On the bus ride home, the team was giddy. It was thrilling to win again—I heard myself laughing—thrilling to make all those plays. Even Rochelle, who was usually quiet, talked and talked. She sat up front with Coach Curry, and, when we pulled into Southie High's parking lot, he stood and congratulated the whole team. He said that the two of us were a model of selflessness, of team spirit, like Cousy and Russell, and I realized he thought we'd planned all those passes, which, I suppose, we had; I mean, she'd told me what to do. I felt this pit in my stomach again. I swear I wanted to kill our coach. My life at school, at home, was hard enough.

Flynn and me hadn't spoken since that night at the Flick, since she'd followed my eyes down the clean, curving line of Elly's powdery cleavage. I'd called once, but when Flynn answered the phone, I'd hesitated. I mean, what was there to say? The first words that came to mind were, Don't leave me. But that was not the kind of thing you said to Flynn. She'd known it was me—was it the quality of my hesitation?—and she'd said, Don't call again, and hung up the phone. In school, if she saw me, she'd cross to the other side of the hall. She wore the SBLA armband now. I'd heard she was with Mike McGuire.

Then one day in March, maybe a week after we beat Dorchester, Rochelle dropped a note at my feet. I was standing at my gym locker after practice, getting my books together, when she passed by very close (it was our habit to keep a wide margin) and dropped a tiny folded paper square. I watched her walk out of the locker room before bending down to retrieve it. The note had been folded over and over again until it was the size of my thumb.

I opened it and read the neat handwriting. It said:

ANN AHERN,
    OUR FRIEND IS LEAVING TOWN. SHE WANTS TO SEE YOU BEFORE SHE GOES. MY AUNT SAYS IF YOU WANT TO SEE HER, YOU SHOULD COME HOME WITH ME. ON THE BUS.

                     ROCHELLE WASHINGTON

I stared at the note. To tell the truth, it was hard to comprehend. Hard to make out. As if the words themselves were a puzzle. Which in a way they were: Take the bus home with Rochelle? In what universe was that? Immediately, I glanced over my shoulder. One of our forwards, the flat-footed Polish girl, sat on a wooden bench collecting her things. Had she seen Rochelle drop the note?

Then I almost fell down under the weight of the sudden realization: Mademoiselle Eugénie wanted to see me! Me, in particular! I groped for a bench. I glanced nervously around the locker room. Ma had a Polish friend, so we were not allowed to use the word *Pollack*. But why was that girl so slow? Everyone else had left. I listened to the sound of my own short breath and read the note again.

It was incredibly short, only four lines, but there were too many things that did not make sense, that were beyond beyond understanding. Mademoiselle Eugénie was leaving town! Was she going back to France? The new rumor at school was that she'd set fire to her car *herself*, in order to get some poor Southie kids in trouble. If she went back to France, that stupid rumor would become fact, would become part of the past. Rochelle's handwriting was tiny, neat; she'd printed in block letters, almost like a typewriter, as if the unbelievable things she'd said would make sense if she just presented them in an orderly way. Honest to God, that note made me light-headed. I mean, it was thrilling, *"our friend,"* it said, as if we *were* friends, as if we shared things in common—ideas, acquaintances, a belief in the impossible. The past. But it was also nauseating. Take the bus home with Rochelle! I didn't know what to do, how to respond, so I gathered up my books and hustled out of the locker room after Rochelle.

When I got outdoors, she was sitting on the cold stone steps in front of the school, waiting for the late bus. I cupped my hands around my mouth to slow my breathing. It was just after four o'clock, but already the sky was getting dark. Carson Beach looked flat and uninviting. I took breath after cold breath. Rochelle sat with her arms wrapped around her knees. She wore a long wool coat, and it spread out like an open clamshell at her feet. Was it true that Blacks couldn't swim? A solitary strand of pink light clung to a group of clouds. I wondered if Carson Beach was facing France. I watched the pink strand back its way out of the sky.

Since the busing, any Blacks who stayed after school for extracurricular activities had to take the late bus at four-thirty. They couldn't miss it. The bus was only for Blacks. It was their last chance to get escorted safely out of Southie. Aside from Rochelle, two other Blacks, boys, ballplayers, I thought, were waiting on the steps. I looked around. I wondered if Rochelle missed Devonne.

A few hundred feet down G Street was a TV news truck, its driver bundled behind the wheel, reading the paper. I hunted for the reporter—their faces were always so well defined, so familiar—but didn't see him. At the edge of the school grounds, just inside the tall, wrought-iron fence that encircled the school, a dozen or so TPF were jawing, their plastic shields piled on the asphalt behind them. One of the cops, a captain, I thought, he had those tassels on his shoulders, stood with some Southie kids. Out of habit, I looked for Flynn. I even looked for her stupid boyfriend, Mike McGuire. I recognized a kid from Old Colony—he was Hap's age—a rash of acne across his face and neck. But then the late Black bus pulled into view, and Rochelle stood up, and my blood raced at the thought that that bus might take me to see Mademoiselle Eugénie.

I started to sweat. I stuffed my damp hands into the front pockets of my jeans. When the door of the bus cranked open, I got this terrible tightness in my chest.

Rochelle stomped her feet. She was a half-dozen steps beneath me. I knew the bus would sit there, idling, for several minutes. I had no idea what to do. Already I had learned that Rochelle held herself back, that she waited. I pulled one of Ma's cigarettes out of my coat pocket. More than anything, I wanted to have my feelings separate, one at a time. Was that too much to ask? I thought Rochelle was waiting for me to say something. This wasn't my idea, I wanted to shout. Ask your aunt— ask your stupid aunt! I looked at the cigarette, which was bent from having ridden without protection in my pocket. I wanted to see Mademoiselle Eugénie, sure. But this was crazy, wrong. The late Black bus.

When I lit the cigarette, Rochelle turned around, frowning. "Coach says we're not supposed to smoke."

I shook my head. "I don't. Not really."

Rochelle squinted at my hand.

"I just puff." I brought the bent cigarette to my lips. "See?" I sucked the smoke in, then blew it out. My hand was chapped from the cold. "I know it looks like I do. But I don't."

"So what's the point?"

I shrugged, sucking in the smoke again.

Her eyes moved to my face. "Wait for me to get on the bus. After a couple minutes, you follow."

I dropped the cigarette and crushed it under my foot. I glanced at the Southie kids, who were still talking to the TPF. "I can't."

"You can't what?"

I puffed out the last of the smoke. "I can't get on that bus."

"You mean, you *won't*. You mean you're scared."

I shook my head. "It's not what you think." I put my hands in my pockets.

"Look. Nobody's gonna bite you."

I shook my head again. She would never understand; Blacks always stuck together. "I mean they won't let me. The monitor. How will I get past the monitor?"

She turned and faced the street, her long back stiff against the cold. "Colleen already thought that out."

"She think of everything, your aunt?"

"The monitor's a friend of ours."

"What?"

"She's a friend of Jean's."

I looked down at my feet. "That's the wrong name for her."

Rochelle glanced over her shoulder. "Say again?"

"Mademoiselle Eugénie. Jeanie. Jean. It's the wrong name for her."

"Man, you've got some Jean-itus, you know that?"

I blushed. "Can I ask you something?"

She was still looking at me.

"Why'd you clock me with the ball?"

"You still mad about that?"

Behind her, the water shone black, metallic-looking. The kids talking to the cops had started to leave; the one with the acne was already gone. "I mean, why'd you start us passing?"

She shrugged. "I got a short attention span," and ran down the steps toward the bus.

The monitor turned out to be the White roommate from Jamaica Plain. She sat in the very first seat and acted like it was completely natural for me to climb on the late Black bus. The driver looked confused, but the monitor had a clipboard and seemed to mark me down, very official-like, and so the driver shrugged and closed the folding door and shifted into gear. The other Blacks, the two boys I'd seen on the steps, stared as I walked down the aisle, their faces full of boredom and hostility. I pretended not to care. I pretended not to be scared by the hostility. In the end, the boredom must have won out, because the boys didn't object, didn't say anything to me or to the monitor.

I stumbled when the bus lurched onto G Street. Rochelle whispered at me to get down. She'd taken the last seat, and I groped my way to the one in front of hers. When I sat, she kicked the back of my seat and said, All the way down, and so I slid onto the floor of the bus, onto my knees, resting my head on the seat cushion. *And blessed is the fruit of thy womb, Jesus.* The floor was wet and dirty.

Rochelle said, "You're traveling incog-Negro now," and laughed.

"What's that supposed to mean?"

"Like *I Spy.*"

I could see the imprint of her knees pressing against the seat back. She laughed some more, her voice high-pitched, silly: tee-hee, tee-hee. I felt my hands and feet get hot. I hated being laughed at. At school, the Blacks were always cracking up, always doubling over. It was bad enough that I'd spent the night in a Black house; now this, now the late Black bus! I couldn't explain it to myself, let alone Ma or Flynn. Of course I wanted to see Mademoiselle Eugénie, but this would be the last straw. Besides, Rochelle's aunt, Colleen Washington, made me nervous. Uncomfortable. She did not talk Black, not at all.

Rochelle kicked the seat again. "Stop pouting. I can hear you pouting all the way back here."

"I'm not pouting."

"Listen, it's a good thing when a Negro calls you a Negro."

"Is that what you called me?"

"You pass the ball like a Negro."

"Coach says I pass like Cousy."

"You pass twice as much as your fat friend did."

"Would you quit—"

"What, she's not fat? She's not a ball hog? You're making some nice passes, that's all I'm saying." She grunted. "Can't take a compliment. If that's not Negro."

I wanted to ask her why she said *Negro* instead of *Black,* but I knew, just using those words, I'd get into trouble.

"Hey, would you look at that? There's a mean-looking White lady hitting some poor Black child on the head with a newspaper."

"You're making that up."

She laughed and kicked the back of my seat again.

I knew she was trying to trap me. To get me to say something bad about Blacks. I said, "How come you're not like this in school?"

"We just crossed the expressway."

I looked up, out the bus window, but all I could see was night sky, the occasional bare treetop.

She said, "I hear you people never leave Southie if you can help it."

"I leave whenever I want."

"Is that right?"

"I got to your aunt's house, didn't I?"

She grunted again, but this time in a not-disapproving way.

"You live there? I mean, with your aunt?"

"Damn these houses are ugly. Big, but ugly. Ever wonder why they paint all these triple-deckers the same damn color?"

A funny taste crept into my mouth. "Where are we now?"

"Dudley Square."

"Where's that?"

"Roxbury."

I had to swallow to keep myself from gasping.

"You bring your passport?"

I thought of those maps the explorers used where the ocean stopped and the sailors sailed off the edge of the earth. I wanted to sit up and look out. I wanted to see. But at the same time, I was, well, reluctant. I remembered Lot's wife. I said, "What's it look like?"

Rochelle was still laughing at her own bad joke. "What kind of a question is that?"

"Is it houses or stores?"

"There's a Thom McCann. A pizza shop."

"What else?"

"See, I was right. You've never even set foot in Roxbury."

"How many times you visit Southie before the busing?"

"That's different."

"Why's that?"

"How am I supposed to get there? Besides, what have you got in South Boston except crazy White people."

I made my voice soft. "Come on."

A siren started up nearby. The sudden wail made my heart pound, then sink. I said, "Please."

She made a clucking sound like she disapproved, but I could tell she liked that I was pleading. I was pleading; I did not know why. She cleared her throat. "There's an old-time luncheonette and a package store, and one of those, what do you call it, medical supply stores. They got three sad-looking toilets in the window, all lined up. Commodes. Now, why go and put those in the window? Why advertise like that?"

"We stopping?"

"Red light."

"There anybody crossing?"

"An old Black lady with a dog, one of those tall, fancy poodles that thinks a lot of itself. Maybe it was white once, but now it's gray. That dog looks as old as Grandma, but still self-satisfied, still preening. The lady's got a church hat on. A brown velvet hat with a brown velvet rose. She's trying to pretend she doesn't see this brother her poodle's sniffing up. He's not her kind. He's tall and skinny, wearing a sheepskin coat. You ever notice that Black people are skinny in a way different from Whites? Less bone. He's all rubber bands. He looks hungry but not poor. He's loving that mangy sheepskin coat. Not Grandma though."

For the rest of the ride, she described what she saw out the window: brick town houses old and well kept, triple-deckers dilapidated and depressed; sickly city trees; Protestant churches, some big, made of pink stone, some storefront; a Spanish church with a flashing neon sign; Chinese restaurants and package stores; a trashed-up, empty house lot; police station; library.

To tell the truth, I liked the sound of her voice. Her particular way of describing. I liked trying to picture what she was saying in my mind's eye. It was soothing. At the same time, I realized it was strange to be driving through Roxbury without actually seeing it. All my life Roxbury had been a no-man's-land, unknowable. Perhaps it should stay that way—what did I know? Besides, who on earth wanted to be Lot's wife? Not me. Forever caught. Not me. Forever standing still.

I inched over to the window and put my mouth at the crack between Rochelle's seat and mine. I tasted salt. I said: "Is Devonne your girlfriend?"

I swear it was someone else's voice.

She kicked the seat back again and again. She kicked the way my baby brother kicks, bicycling her legs. She kicked until I lost my balance, my head and shoulders pitching me forward, into the side of the bus, the two of us laughing.

When I caught my breath, I climbed off the dirty floor, onto the seat. I lay with my head below the window, staring up at the stained ceiling of the bus. I tucked my knees into my chest. "I mean, *was* your girlfriend. Because you broke up, didn't you?"

The bus stopped and let the boys off. I listened to it start again; the driver shifted into first then second, the bus groaning. We waited at a stop sign or a red light, I could only guess. As we made the long, slow, awkward, arcing turn onto whatever street or avenue, I realized this was my first-ever, in-person conversation about girls.

I used my pleading voice again. "Come on. Why'd you two break up?"

She sat up and pressed her head against the back of my seat cushion. I could see the impression the crown of her head made, and I had the urge to reach out and touch it.

She said quietly, "Did you know that Bob Cousy used to travel incog-Negro?"

Now I sat up. I leaned forward and peered over the back of the seat. She was looking down at the bus's dirty floor.

"He rode with Russell in the Negro car of the train."

"What train?"

"When they went south, for games. It was still Jim Crow then. The Black players had to ride in the Negro car."

"The NBA players?"

She looked up at me and nodded. She wore that same closed-over expression she'd had when I'd stepped outside Southie High. "Cousy sat with Bill Russell the whole way."

I was not sure how to respond—to act surprised, or *not* surprised—I was not sure which she would prefer. So I just held my face still.

She nodded again, and this time I saw that her expression was not closed-over, it was reserved, like she was waiting for something.

16

M¹ second visit to Mademoiselle Eugénie's
house, Rochelle led me up the front stairs. I had thought we
would sit in the Black living room—me and Mademoiselle
Eugénie—I had thought we would converse there, the two of
us balanced on the yellow couch.

Instead, Rochelle opened the door to Mademoiselle Eugénie's bedroom. "Jean's not here." She stepped inside. "She's
with my aunt. At some meeting." Rochelle spun around, opening her arms wide, like she was offering something. "They're
always at some meeting those two."

I hesitated.

"Come on in. It's all right. Jean lets me hang in her room
when she's not here."

"So you *do* live in this house?"

In the middle of the room, Rochelle pulled on a metal
chain to turn on the overhead light. Now the dark windows
showed her long, loping reflection, the dandelion Afro. She
fingered the chain. "Since my mama found out about me and
Devonne."

"When was that?"

Rochelle shrugged, then frowned.

I wanted to ask a million questions, but the frown was not inviting. Instead, I stepped inside, eyed the familiar single bed with the familiar plaid blanket, the undecorated cardboard dresser, the child's desk and chair. I thought about the last time, when I was trespassing. Everything was different now; now Rochelle was here. She crossed over to Mademoiselle Eugénie's desk and peered out the window. It was not simply that the room was sparse: There was a sadness, a lack of pleasure. I closed my eyes and pictured the strange French penmanship. *Chère maman,* one of her letters had said. I opened my eyes. "Is she going back to France?"

Rochelle shook her head. "Not to France."

I glanced at the closet. I had the urge to open the door, to see the tight French clothes. "Where's she going then?"

Rochelle sighed in this exaggerated way. "It's hard to explain."

There was a way she was acting—I didn't like it. She picked a book off the seat of the child's chair and pretended to read it. She was acting like Mademoiselle Eugénie belonged to her. Honestly, I wished we were back on the bus, just the two of us. Riding through Roxbury.

Rochelle held up the book. "Jean asked me to give you this."

"No way."

"Way." She nodded

My heart sort of flipped—a present from Mademoiselle Eugénie! Why on earth? I took the book from Rochelle's outstretched hand. The cover had no picture, just the title in big block letters, graffiti style. *The Fire Next Time,* it said. There were flames shooting out from behind the fat letters. On the back was a picture of a Black man, the writer I figured. But why had she left it for me? He was very dark-skinned with a broad Black nose and big runny eyes that took up half his face, like a frog. He was smoking a cigarette. He was ugly, but at the same time, I didn't know, sad or something. Unsure. Which made the ugliness almost delicate.

I flipped the book open and read the first sentence I came across: "I underwent, during the summer that I became fourteen, a prolonged religious crisis."

"That's strange," I said. "That's strange." I found myself getting excited. "I had a religious crisis myself, when I was twelve." I glanced around the room. I had the weird sensation that Mademoiselle Eugénie was watching me. I said to Rochelle, "Have you read this book?"

"Sure."

"Have you ever? Do you believe in God?"

"What's not to believe?" She sat down on the child's desk, her back to the windows. The room was big, almost empty, with hardly any furniture, but still, Rochelle looked confined somehow.

In his photograph, the Black man, the writer, was glancing off to the side, smiling at someone we couldn't see. To tell the truth, he reminded me just the littlest bit of Mademoiselle Eugénie. They were the same dark color. She was like a beautiful version of him: his ugliness reversed, turned inside out. Or, I guess you could say, she was his beauty made manifest. It was a word I hadn't thought of in a long time, a Catholic word. I must have looked puzzled because Rochelle said, quietly, like she was answering a question: "She's not who you think she is."

"What?"

"Jean's not just some French teacher."

Now I shrugged, pretending not to care, my stomach leaping to the back of my throat. "Who is she then?"

Rochelle put her feet on the seat of the chair. "Those meetings she goes to with my aunt?"

I nodded.

She leaned forward, elbows on knees. "One hundred percent *I Spy*."

"I don't know what that means."

She frowned. "Keep your mouth shut?"

"I guess."

She shook her head. "You gotta do better than guess."

"Okay. How about—who'm I gonna tell?"

She chewed the inside of her cheek. "Jean's going underground."

"What?"

Rochelle lowered her voice. "You heard me." She made a tunneling motion with her hand. "Underground."

I whispered back, "Like Patty Hearst?"

"Exactly."

"But why? She didn't do anything wrong."

Rochelle shook her head. "No, she didn't. Not here. She didn't do anything wrong in this country." She raised her eyebrows.

Now my heart was pounding. That didn't make any sense. If I understood correctly. If I understood what Rochelle was suggesting, implying. Finally, I said, "But why would she go underground here for doing something wrong someplace else?"

"It's complicated."

"You keep saying that!"

"Well, it is!"

"You mean you have no fucking idea! You mean they won't tell you!"

She stood on the chair. "Look, did it ever occur to you? Isn't it, you know, something of a coincidence that she came to South Boston High now, in the middle of all this, this, whatever it is?"

"Trouble."

"Trouble," she snorted. "That's what you people call it?"

Then I remembered the postcard of the Black man in the French beret. The one who sat enthroned on the wicker chair, holding a spear. I remembered how mad I'd been when I'd found it on Mademoiselle Eugénie's writing desk. I said, "You ever go to one of those meetings?"

She shook her head.

"I mean, what do they do there?"

She slumped back down. "Colleen says I'm too young. That I have to be eighteen. Otherwise it would be like *she* was making the decision for me."

To tell the truth, I was amazed by my capacity to forget what I'd already learned. What I already knew.

Rochelle stared at her big basketball feet. "The only decision Colleen ever makes is too keep me cooped up, inside. She's overprotective because of Mama. She says Mama will kill her if anything happens to me." She clucked her tongue. "But nothing ever happens to me." Rochelle hopped down from the writing table. "I don't want to wait until I'm eighteen. By then, I'll have missed everything. Do you ever get the feeling?" She looked around, suddenly excited. "Civil Rights is over! I missed all that! The Freedom Rides—the lunch counters!" She grabbed my shoulder. "*We* missed all that! Just by a couple of years." She shook her head. "Okay, okay, maybe more than a couple of years, but still. What I'm saying is, I don't want to miss what's happening now. You follow?"

I nodded, but to tell the truth, I had no idea what she was talking about. The busing?

She still had a hand on my shoulder, and now she squeezed it . "Look, take a drive with me." She licked her lips. Her face lost its old-soul quality. "I know where she is. I overheard my aunt talking. I know where Jean is right this second."

I frowned. "I thought you said she was at some meeting."

She released my shoulder.

"You lied to me!"

"Not exactly."

"Then what, exactly?"

She smiled, pinching her fingers together. "I tweaked the truth."

"You think this is some kind of joke! For Christ's sake! You made me take the late Black bus!"

"Oh, keep your panties on! You survived, didn't you? You're still here! Still White! Besides, I gave you that book, didn't I? Jean asked me to give it to you. She's not far from here. We could drive there tomorrow. We could take my aunt's car."

"Take your aunt's car!"

"She won't miss it! She never uses it on Saturdays. She's at one of her meetings all day!"

"Does she hate White people?"

Rochelle scrunched up her face. "Aunt Colleen?"

I shook my head. "Mademoiselle Eugénie."

She jumped in the air. "Aren't you listening to me?" She actually jumped up and down. "Haven't you heard a word I've said? Take the cotton out of your ears, girl!" She was shouting. "Jean wants to see you before she goes. That's what she said. I swear to God. Jean wants to see you before she leaves town for good. Now, are you going to come with me or not?"

I stared at the book in my hand. It was written in English, not French, but somehow it was a kind of code, a signal from Mademoiselle Eugénie, but I didn't know what the signal meant. On the back cover, the man's eyes were as big as moons. The more I looked, the more I could see the sorrow there. The suffering. But then I noticed something I hadn't seen before. Tucked inside the very last page was a piece of paper, one of the burned letters I'd written to Mademoiselle Eugénie! I couldn't believe it. She'd gotten those stupid letters after all! My face got unbelievably hot. I glanced at Rochelle but she was still talking loud, still trying to convince me.

"What I'm saying is, she wants to see us both. She's not like my aunt. Jean says young people are the future."

The letter was less than a half a page, its burned edges still coming away in my hands. My handwriting looked looping and unfamiliar, girlish, like I'd been much younger when I'd written the letter. I could make out two longish words: *designation* and *hyperbole.* I blushed even harder then. Obviously, obviously, I was showing off. Someday my skin was going to burst into flames of embarrassment!

I looked up at Rochelle. Her face was bright, expectant, almost pleading, but in a forceful way. I realized she wore the same expression the day she threw the ball at my head. I hadn't registered it then. The day she'd singled me out by humiliating me. In the locker room, when I shoved her against the metal stall, her face had had the same intense expectancy. I got this tingling sensation all over my skin. Not quite déjà vu, but a rush of old feelings. Was this why she'd singled me out? I opened the book again. The Black man wrote: "For this was the beginning of our burning time . . ." Our burning time? Our burning time? I felt a familiar panic in my stomach and throat. I glanced at Rochelle. She looked lit from inside. There was a word for that.

She said, "Jean believes only young people are capable of radical change."

"Radical what?"

Rochelle raised her eyebrows.

Incandescent. It was the same word in French as in English. *Incandescent.*

17

Sometimes, the things you think will be the hardest turn out to be the easiest, a lark, like taking the aunt's car. She left a spare key in the plastic flowerpot that sat on the kitchen table. *Voilà.* She also left money there, something Rochelle did not expect, wedged under the pretend grass of the flowerpot, five ten-dollar bills.

Then, vice versa, the things you think won't be much trouble turn out to be the big deal: Rochelle didn't drive a stick shift. Turns out Mademoiselle Eugénie was on the Cape, in Provincetown, which was pretty far out, on the actual tip. I'd only driven standard that one time with Danny Flynn. At first it was stop-start, stop-start, all the way down the street. Then I remembered what Danny had taught me, to ease up on the clutch; I remembered the slow release, the car like a seesaw. I remembered the ball of the stick shift hard and slippery and satisfying in my hand.

Turns out Provincetown was at the end of the earth, at land's end. I thought it was a weird place to hide from the police—with your back to the water. A weird place to go underground. Wasn't the Cape below sea level?

That night, at home in my bed, I had a terrible dream

about Mademoiselle Eugénie. She was swimming all the way to France. I was standing on a large rock, at the edge of the water. I kept shouting: *But Blacks don't swim! Blacks don't swim!* She couldn't hear me. She swam without putting her bouffant in the water, her dark elbows pointing up suddenly, like fins.

The dream made me anxious. Anxious to go. We took off in the morning as soon as the aunt left the house. I was already there, in JP, waiting across the street, crouched behind a parked car. I watched her walk down the street, serious, purposeful, a compact version of Rochelle. She left a few minutes after nine o'clock. She took the subway, the orange line that I had just now ridden on for the first time.

In the car, as we drove, I told Rochelle about Laura Miskinis. The words poured out of my mouth. I told her how Laura had looked that day in ninth grade, our first day at Southie High, standing at the bottom of the stairs by the metal shop, acting confused, asking if I knew where her next class was—room 205?—geography? And how we'd laughed at the thought of her getting lost on the way to geography. And how her pink ear had felt to the tip of my tongue. The waxy taste. In the car I turned incredibly red; I couldn't help it; I had never told anyone. By then we'd driven all the way through Franklin Park and Mattapan. We were in Milton, where my cousins lived, about to get on the expressway south, and Rochelle said, without looking at me, her eyes out the window watching the cars zoom past: "You sure can blush."

What turned out to be difficult was telling Ma I would not be home to take Timmy to the library. It's not exactly that I thought telling Ma would be easy. It's that I was so distracted, so preoccupied: I was thinking about Rochelle. I was wondering what on earth I was doing driving in a car with a girl from Roxbury. A borrowed car. I'd seen this movie once, a Black and White chained together, trying to escape the South. At first, they hated each other's guts. Sidney Poitier played the Black.

He was very well spoken, everyone said, very articulate. Tony Curtis played the White, a Southern redneck. Ma said he was prettier than a girl. Too pretty. At first, they could hardly stand each other.

But there was another movie that I couldn't stop thinking about: scientists walking down, down, trying to find the exact center of the earth. Down, down, I don't know why, but I remembered their silver backpacks.

I said to Rochelle, "You ever see this movie called *Journey to the Center of the Earth*?"

She shook her head no.

Underground was not a place, I knew that, it was a way of living, of hiding from the police. Still, the movie had made it clear: Going underground, to the center of the earth, was one thing, was difficult; but coming back was another. Coming back was pretty much impossible. I wondered what she'd done, Mademoiselle Eugénie.

To Rochelle I said, "I have to call my mother."

We pulled over to the side of the road, to a rest area. Just a half-moon road with some portable johns and a pay phone. Rochelle stayed inside the car. She found a map tucked into the side of the passenger door and opened it.

Outside, I straddled the door of the phone booth. I faced the thin woods behind the rest area. It was cold, so I pulled up the scratchy collar of my jean jacket.

Ma answered the phone immediately. "Ann?"

I said, "Yeah, Ma. It's me." I had to shout over the sounds of the expressway.

"What's that noise? Where in God's name are you?"

"You wouldn't believe me if I told you."

"I don't know what to believe from you anymore." Her voice was animated, intense. When I'd left that morning, she hadn't gotten home yet from work. "It's as if I don't know my own daughter."

"Don't say that, Ma."

She sucked on her cigarette. "I woke up one morning and she's a stranger. A complete stranger."

"Listen, Ma—"

"How long have you been lying to me?"

"Lying?"

"Yes, lying." She blew out the smoke.

The cord to the receiver was way too short. I kept pulling on it to lengthen it, but each time I pulled, the cord yanked me farther into the phone booth.

"I understand you took the late Black bus."

"Jesus fucking Christ."

"Watch your talk."

"Could fucking Southie get any smaller?"

"I mean it. I'll knock that talk right out of your mouth."

"Who told you?"

But she didn't answer. Instead, I listened to her smoke. On the ground were those little asphalt pebbles, not actual rocks, just clusters of tar. I kicked at them and watched them spray. "Listen, Ma, I'm not going to be able to take Timmy to the library. I'm going. Well, I'm going to visit this friend of mine. I didn't want you to worry."

She laughed. "How considerate of you to call. I'm going to tell all my friends what a considerate daughter I have."

"Listen, I can't stay on long. I just wanted to let you know. I'll be back, well, kind of late."

"What I can't understand, Ann, what I find hard to fathom is why you'd rather spend your time with a bunch of niggers than be here with us. With your own family."

I looked over at Rochelle. She had opened the passenger door and sat with her feet on the ground, the map spread open on her lap. To tell the truth, nigger was a word I had heard every day of my life in South Boston. I'd heard it so many times the word was weightless. Meaningless. Rochelle bent forward, studying the map, her long fingers tracing an invisible route. A nonword. A gust of wind blew her soft Afro away from her face, and she looked suddenly younger, unprotected, suddenly eager, like Timmy.

"That's it, isn't it?" Ma's voice was low. "You'd rather be with them, than be here with us?"

Just not in our house: We had never used that particular word in our house.

"What I can't understand is, why you treat total strangers better than you treat your own family."

Ma had a way—always, always—of making you choose sides.

I said, "Look, I gotta go."

"Just a minute. I want you to explain something to me. Would you do that? I'm going to tell you a little story; I'm going to describe a recent event here at home; and I want you to explain it to me, because I'm just not sophisticated enough to understand it."

I stepped inside the phone booth. There was a terrible pit in my stomach, and I wanted to hang up the phone, but couldn't. Then she told me how one of our neighbors, Mrs. Sullivan, had come to see her at work. She came to explain what every person in Southie High knew but Ma didn't: about Laura Miskinis in the ninth grade. Mrs. Sullivan was the mother of the kid who'd seen me climb the late Black bus, the kid with the terrible acne. She told Ma how, after letting me put my tongue in her ear for a full five minutes, Laura Miskinis had screamed. And how the metal shop teacher, Mr. Lapides, had come running, abandoning his classroom. Even now, even standing there by the side of the road, I could hear the high whine of those deadly metal machines. At the time, the headmaster had wanted to tell Ma, but because Lapides had hit me, had knocked me down, which was against the law, he couldn't.

There was a long, loud silence on the phone. Then a ringing in my ears. I had the taste in my mouth that you get just before throwing up.

Ma said, "Well? Can you *enlighten* me?"

"When did you—"

"Mrs. Sullivan said that if it was her daughter, she'd want to know."

"But that doesn't prove—"

Ma said, "*Any*thing but this."

I said, stupidly, "It's not what you think."

"I'm just not sophisticated enough."

Always, always, she made you choose one side of yourself over the rest.

"If you're not home in an hour, don't bother coming back."

I hung up the phone.

PART FOUR

Traveling
Incog-Negro

18

We stop at a pancake house just over the Bourne Bridge. The restaurant is A-shaped, its slanted roof the brightest possible blue. When we leap out of the car, the sound of our sneakers on the clamshell parking lot is loud. We are hopped up, excited. I can feel the adrenaline. I watch Rochelle restrain herself from running across the parking lot. I watch my sneakers walk across the millions of broken seashells, trailing Rochelle.

It seems that I am the star of a movie about my own life. I feel the heat of the camera lights, which are so bright I cannot see the crew hiding behind them. But I can hear them whispering, moving about. The movie is about a White girl from South Boston who becomes friends with a Black, a girl from Roxbury. In the restaurant scene, the White waitress looks up from where she is standing behind the counter, her pretty face not even trying to disguise her surprise. In one hand, she holds a coffeepot, in the other, plastic menus as long as her arm. She does not drop the coffeepot. For a second, the White waitress reminds the main character (me!) of someone else (Elly!): She has dyed black hair and big boobs that strain against the zipper of her orange-and-blue uniform. On the collar of the uniform she wears an enormous button that says: Ask me what a fudgeanna is!

Momentarily, because of the button, I feel sorry for her. And out of that sympathy and recognition comes the surprising desire to undo her zipper, to watch the big boobs fall out. I feel horny and embarrassed and turn as red as the roof here is blue; Rochelle sees, and I worry she has mistaken my reaction for something else. My embarrassment makes me hate the waitress now.

We sit at the counter to save time. Rochelle orders the Big Breakfast, which is a lot of food: eggs, pancakes, sausage, and toast. In her pocket is the money her aunt had tucked into the flowerpot. The number of bills is few—only five tens—but the amount of money itself seems huge. Out of proportion. It makes us dizzy: Not only are we traveling together, driving in a car unsupervised by any adult, we are rich. Rich! The waitress puts down her coffeepot and writes our order with great concentration; she seems to write many more words than Big Breakfast. When I say I'll have the same thing, she sneaks peeks at the two of us before hurrying away. It occurs to me that she is jealous. Despite this realization (because of it?), I don't hate her any less.

For the first time in my life, I can feel everything that is happening to me: every molecule of air that brushes my skin; every stare or frown from every White customer; every movement toward and away from us; every smile and grimace of Rochelle's. But instead of being disturbed by this rush of feeling, I am—what's the word?—enlarged by it. As an actress in the movie of my life, I will be known for my ability to contain and express many feelings at once.

Now the horniness is free-floating, huge. Out of proportion.

Rochelle is an actress too; I am only just learning how talented. In school, she had seemed quiet, reserved, her face a flat wall that she hid behind. But here now, I watch her face, and it is amazingly mobile, unpredictable.

She points to my cup of tea, her chin poking forward with disapproval. "How many sugars you put in that?"

"What's the difference?"

Rochelle shakes her head, clucks her tongue. She is drinking coffee, no cream, no sugar. Ever since we climbed into her aunt's car she's been acting incredibly cool, incredibly sophisticated, like what we're doing is no big deal. Like it won't change her. She takes a sip of the muddy coffee, and I see her nostrils flare, then quiver.

I say, "You're full of crap."

And suddenly she doubles up, laughing, the coffee spurting out her nose and mouth.

The pretty waitress looks over—she is raising her soft white arm to place our order slip in the open window where the cook can see it—and frowns at Rochelle with disgust. Now we both double over, cracking up. Suddenly I am on the inside of something I've been watching from the outside my whole life. We laugh and laugh. Heads turn in our direction. It feels good to laugh. It feels good to be on the inside, at last.

Back in the car, Rochelle says, "Follow the rotary almost all the way around." She points to a line she has drawn herself on the map. "We want Route Six. We'll drive along the canal and then Route Six kind of hooks to the right." On top of the map rests her place mat from the pancake house, which is a tourist map of Cape Cod.

I say, "You leave a tip?"

She shakes her head. "I asked her what a FUDGEANNA is, and she didn't even know."

I laugh so hard my face starts to hurt.

"If a Black girl did that, you know she'd be getting fired."

I beg her to stop, stop, stop.

Now the horniness is not free-floating, but pointed, sharp. My side aches from laughing so hard.

I roll down the window to get some air. Aunt Colleen's car is a Duster, red, with a squishy interior whose vinyl is beat up, torn. The ripped vinyl has been patched with red duct tape, which is not the same color red. The stick shift is a skinny shaft with a shiny black ball on top. I practice shifting, making the "H." With my free hand, I finger the ache in my side.

Rochelle says, "From here, it's about an hour and a half to Provincetown."

"You know the house she's staying at?"

She nods. "These friends of my aunt's."

I adjust my rearview mirror, settle into my seat. The Duster's two front seats are separate, not fully bucket seats, but not one long banquette either. Even though there are moments when I do not particularly like Rochelle's attitude—know-it-all, show-off—I realize no one has ever treated me the way she has: like I can get from point A to point B; like I have the wherewithal to move through the world as an adult. It is more than trust, it is acknowledgment. A wave of gratitude overtakes me; my eyes sting. And then this gratitude makes me feel even more horny, if that were possible, which, if you'd asked me a minute ago, I'd have said was not.

I bite my lip, hard, wanting to feel something else, some other sensation. But now every feeling—gratitude, pain, excitement— gets translated into the same insistent thing. I can't stand how overwhelming it is. How grinding. I want to climb out of the car, but can't because we're about to go. I realize this is the feeling people are trying to describe when they say: I was climbing out of my own skin. To distract myself, to distract Rochelle, I point to a sign at the entrance to the bridge: "Check that out."

The sign is white, with big blue letters. DESPERATE? it says. CALL THE SAMARITANS. It gives a number.

Rochelle looks at the sign, then at the color rising on my neck. I can feel her eyes on my skin. She says, "It's like a stain or something."

I think ridiculously of jumping off the bridge.

She says, "You feeling desperate already?"

The answer ripples through my body. When I turn, she kisses me on the mouth.

19

NOTHING THAT HAPPENED NEXT WENT THE WAY I'D pictured it. For one, I'd always pictured Laura Miskinis with all her clothes off. Laura Miskinis with me on top, kissing her, touching her big, White boobs. But Rochelle wouldn't take her clothes off, plus I already knew her boobs were small, even if I didn't get to see them. Small and brown. Black. What exact color were the nipples?

I knew it was a prejudiced thing to say that Blacks smelled different than Whites. I knew that it was. When Rochelle shrugged off her coat—one long arm got stuck, and she had to shrug and shrug again—her Black smell lifted off her skin and filled the car; it was a little bit smoky, a little bit scratching at the back of my throat. And bitter, like pennies. And thick, like oil. To tell the truth, it turned me off. My mouth was dry, parched. When she put her tongue inside, I thought, that's a Black tongue. Black lips. I couldn't stop thinking those thoughts. At first, it felt too much, I couldn't swallow, couldn't breathe, I wanted to push her off; but then, when our tongues touched, my body and mouth opened at once. Now her tongue was plush, thrilling. I wanted it inside, inside, farther, farther. We kissed and kissed. Who knew what kissing did? Not me. I had never kissed anyone.

After a while, Rochelle pulled my sweatshirt up, over my head, like she was going to take it off. But instead, she left it there, covering my face, so I couldn't see. I couldn't see! Then she put her mouth on my boob, and I felt almost hysterical, like an animal. Like weeping. I was panting like a dog. I could smell my own smell now.

The long fingers of her hand found my other, rigid nipple. The feelings rushed at me, and I wanted to scream, to stop. But also, I wanted to take the sweatshirt off. I wanted to see her *on* me. Honest to God, even as we did those things, it was hard to comprehend, hard to fathom. At last, when I was able to see, her face was so close to mine, there was only half a mouth, a single eye—wild, brimming, intent on something. I glimpsed, underneath her chin, a slice of collar bone. If you really loved a girl, I had thought, you didn't think of her in pieces, you thought of her as a whole. But I'd been wrong. Wrong.

Later, she went to pull my pants off, and I looked over her shoulder, afraid that someone might see into the car—we were still in the parking lot—see me lying there, exposed. But the windows had fogged up: We were making our own weather. In school, you always heard about finger fucking like it was some sort of pathetic, shameful thing; I kept twisting and twisting away from her. When her finger found the opening, my entire body sort of seized. And seized again. She put more fingers in. I gripped them hard. Farther, farther. As far inside as possible. She put her other hand inside my mouth, and I thought maybe the fingers in my pussy and the fingers that I sucked might come together, touch.

After, when I tried to take Rochelle's pants off, she wouldn't let me. I pushed her away, into her own seat, and said, "Come on, it's not fair."

She climbed back and breathed: "It's not supposed to be."

I felt humiliated, enthralled.

That was how we made our way up the Cape, Route 6. I

mean, we'd drive for a while, then the feeling would sort of build up, and we'd pull off to the side of the road. No matter how far we went, there was no finishing, no end. When she climbed on top, I felt the hard bone above her pussy touching mine. She pushed and pushed. After the rotary at Orleans, we stopped in an empty parking lot, behind a clump of trees. The pine trees got skimpier and more twisted the farther we drove. In Wellfleet, we parked behind a Monopoly-sized motel, six or seven shuttered boxes set in a row. All the buildings were weather-beaten, gray, leeched of color. I thought, probably, I should have been interested in the scenery, in what was happening outside the car. I thought, probably, things would finish, end, if I got to put my fingers inside Rochelle.

My pussy bone ached.

When the sun began to sink, I got that prick of dread you get toward the end of the day. And I realized I had started to dread seeing Mademoiselle Eugénie again.

20

Truro was the last town before Provincetown. Suddenly there was a gentle hill and we sloped down it, and then the sea grass and pine trees were gone, and there were sand dunes to our right, piles and piles of soft triangles, and flat water that looked more like a lake, not ocean, and we could just as easily have been on the moon, the landscape was so far out, so strange, except for these tiny white cottages in a long row to our left. The cottages were boarded up but had bright green shutters. They faced water, the ocean for real. It was blue-gray with mist coming off it, rising like rain in the wrong direction. The gray sky had ripples like the water.

Rochelle leaned forward, her arms on the dashboard. "This left, here."

I put my blinker on. I had wanted to point to the rising rain; I had wanted to mention the rippled sky.

Up ahead, a bunch of houses and buildings was set against the curving waterline. The houses looked almost accidental, as if someone had tossed them there, like so many marbles, and at the same time, permanent, like they'd grown naturally out of the sand. Almost against my will, I thought of Ma, who loved the water. I thought of Hap and Timmy and the twins.

Rochelle played with the lock on the passenger door. Her long face looked horsey again. Inside my shirt, my nipples tensed. I had always thought that after sex, the other person would become more familiar, not less.

We drove into town on Commercial Street, the main drag. The whole town was washed-out, deserted-looking, the windows of all the shops and houses boarded-up. I mean, shop after boarded-up shop. That place was empty, not a soul on the street. We passed a wooden dock that jutted out, lonesome, into the water. We passed signs for Pilgrim Monument, Pilgrim Beach. That town was empty like the wild wild West. We passed a closed-up bank and church and photo store. I bet, in the summer, people took lots of pictures of themselves on the beach. I bet that store was jam-packed, the store and the streets. The contrast—even if it was only in my mind's eye—was strange. Disconcerting. I swear you could feel the hum of all the bodies that had left. A pit in my stomach opened, flooding.

I pointed to a sign for the Mayflower Restaurant. I said, "Provincetown must be a big Pilgrim town."

Rochelle rolled down her window and looked out, turning her head to follow the sign. Her Afro brushed the roof of the car. "Miriam says the Pilgrims came here first, before they stepped on Plymouth Rock."

"Who's Miriam?"

"The people who are taking care of Jean."

To tell the truth, I didn't care if I ever saw Mademoiselle Eugénie again. I just wanted to drive with Rochelle, it didn't matter where. I just wanted to stay in that car. I said, "Massachusetts has quite a number of them. Pilgrim towns, I mean. Plymouth. Salem. Old Sturbridge."

Rochelle sat back in her seat, shook her head. "Salem's witches not Pilgrims. Witches."

"Same thing."

"Nuh-uh."

Suddenly I wanted to cry.

Rochelle glanced at the map, still open on her lap. She seemed far away, distracted. "We're looking for Pleasant Street." She frowned. "We have to hurry. We stopped too much. We have to see Jean and get back before my aunt gets out of her meeting."

"We could just turn around."

She shook her head.

I hated how panicked I felt. "How does your aunt know Mademoiselle Eugénie?"

Rochelle shrugged.

I stopped at an intersection, bit my lip. "It's not my fault that we're late."

She looked out the window. "Didn't say that it was."

We took the next right, then crossed another main drag, parallel to the first, but farther away from the water. The houses were close together, almost touching. Halfway down Pleasant, we turned onto a dirt road with only three houses, these spaced farther apart, one a trailer set on concrete. We stopped at the last one, a small, gray-shingled house, with worn trim, and climbed out of the car. The driveway was the same sandy dirt as the road.

When I stood, I saw that the rippled sky had opened out, until it was not just above us, but all around us, on every side. I looked across the roof of the car; Rochelle's billowy hair was a reverse halo against the gray. And I thought to myself, We're drowning in sky! And I had the urge to tell Rochelle that, to say, *We're drowning in sky,* because, well, because it sounded so poetical and surely this was a poetical place, with the water and the rippled sky and all; but also, because I had the sensation of drowning, of sinking farther and farther below some invisible line; I had the feeling, I couldn't shake it, that everything was about to change.

I said: "I'm traveling incog-Negro now."

She came around to my side of the car.

I tried to keep the panic out of my voice. "I'm like those White girls in the projects with Black babies who nobody even sees as White anymore."

She brought her hand to my cheek. Her eyes were liquid brown, a crescent of white along the bottom rims; the white made the brown part look bigger, wetter, softer. She smiled. "Don't worry," she said. Her knuckles grazed my cheek. "You're definitely still White."

I wanted her to keep touching my face. I said, "Why'd you break up with Devonne?"

Her voice was soft. "I told you already."

I shook my head.

Gently, gently, she pulled my hair. "I got a short attention span."

Right then, the front door opened.

She dropped her hand.

A tall Black man stepped outside and threw both arms in the air. "Shelle!"

She turned around.

He was big and bulky, but in a soft, rather than muscular, way. "What a surprise!" He hopped down the stairs two at a time and wrapped his arms around her. He was medium color. "What a surprise!" he repeated.

Rochelle said, "Hey."

"Miriam know you're here?"

Rochelle shook her head.

He pounded her back with his wide, flat hands. "Sister Shelle!" He pulled her inside, then came back for me. "You too, sister, come on in."

I acted natural.

"Name's Alphonse."

I shook his outstretched hand.

Rochelle said, "That's Ann Ahern."

My face, my lips, my ears burned red.

"Welcome. Welcome, Ann Ahern. You ever been to Provincetown?"

I shook my head.

"You're in for a treat, then. A real treat." He steered us down the hallway, one hand on Rochelle's neck, one at my elbow. I acted like this happened every day. The house was beautiful, wood planks on all the surfaces, not just the floor, but the walls too, shiny with shellac. The wood was butter color, with black swirls, like little universes, or galaxies, inside each plank. On the one hand, I felt this strangeness, the strangeness of the trip, of being in (another) Black house, of meeting a strange Black man: me, Ann Ahern, a girl from South Boston. But on the other, was Rochelle, her incredible, well, proximity. I mean, even when my head was turned, I knew exactly where she was. How many steps.

In the living room, Alphonse ducked a hanging paper lamp shade shaped like a beehive. "Miriam'll be thrilled," he said to Rochelle. "She's at work." Then to me, apologetic: "I'm always at home. A painter."

I nodded like I understood.

We stood around a blocky couch and chairs, a driftwood coffee table. He took our coats, motioned for us to sit. Then I saw the speckles on the backs of his hands. He said, "Can I get you all a drink?"

Plus, on every wall, impossible to miss, was the same large painting.

Rochelle sat down on the soft-cube couch. I stood, arms folded across my chest, and tried not to stare at the paintings. At the center of each one was a naked Black. A female.

"We got beer, wine. Vodka and OJ?"

I felt the color rising in my cheeks.

Rochelle said, "Jean here?"

He shook his head.

She smiled. "A tonic would be good."

I looked down, stomped one foot. I wanted to drain the redness out of my face. I had only ever seen naked Blacks in porno magazines.

Alphonse looked at me and smiled, to ask my drink, and I nodded, and he smiled again, bigger, his whole face—mouth, nose, eyes—turning up. His hair was in braids, like Aunt Colleen's, but longer, past his shoulders, and thicker, more elaborate: Little bits of fabric were woven in. He looked more like a friendly lion than a man who painted naked females all day long. He repeated, "A tonic would be good," saving me from speech.

When he left, Rochelle stood and examined the paintings up close. In every one, the naked female was extremely realistic-looking, almost like a photograph, but, at the same time, she was cartoonish too. Part superhero. Part fantastic wife. The breasts were like missiles. She was running in the paintings. She ran *at* you, muscles glistening. The background was the checkerboard pattern of a kitchen floor: red and gold, orange and blue, purple and green, only the colors were brighter than a kitchen floor, richer, like syrup.

I said, "Is that his wife, what's her name?" The nipples were red, bursting.

"Miriam?" Rochelle shook her head.

To tell the truth, those paintings made me nervous. They seemed like a joke. A joke on me: I had thought before, in Jamaica Plain, that I had been in a Black house. But I was wrong, wrong. This was Blackness to the nth degree. Besides, they made me think of the body I had not seen—I mean, in the car. I felt teased. I said, "Is this some kind of a joke?"

"You see anybody laughing?"

Just then Alphonse returned with the tonics.

I felt cotton-headed, confused. I said, "Alphonse, can you tell us where Mademoiselle Eugénie is?"

"Who?"

Rochelle rolled her eyes. "That's what she calls Jean."

Alphonse looked at me and tilted his head. He smiled like he hadn't really seen me before. "Name's Alphonse, but people call me Big Al. Jean's with Miriam." He handed me an orange tonic. Another to Rochelle. "They'll be home soon. Any minute."

Rochelle nodded. "We can't stay long. Jean wanted—she asked me to bring Ann before she left town. But my aunt wants us back tonight." She cleared her throat. She was staring at the painting behind the couch. "I like that one there," she pointed.

Big Al bobbed his head up and down, obviously delighted. He squinted at the painting. In it, a reddish-brown butterfly with black spots covered the entire pubic area. He said, "I call it *Double Aphrodite.*"

"She's cool," Rochelle said, "Kind of psychedelic. Kind of super-duper nigger style." She laughed.

He laughed.

I took a sip of my orange tonic. I wanted to laugh, but couldn't. The tonic tasted terribly sweet. The more sophisticated Rochelle acted, the more ridiculous I felt. The spotted butterfly seemed to emphasize that every other bush was bare. I thought of Flynn and my mother. It was impossible to picture them here. Impossible. I ground my teeth together, picturing them. The thing was, Rochelle and me had only just become— whatever it was. I didn't want to lose her yet. I tried to think of something sophisticated to say, something smart. ASK ME WHAT A FUDGEANNA IS!

Rochelle said, "Why double Aphrodite?"

Big Al leaned over the couch. He made a soft sound, of satisfaction, deep in his throat. "The butterfly. They call her *Speyeria Aphrodite* 'cause she's so beautiful."

Rochelle nodded. "She's definitely that."

I coughed. "I thought Aphrodite was, you know, the Greek goddess of love?"

"That's right, that's right. She's the goddess of love and beauty and what they call rapture."

Rapture?

Big Al pointed at the butterfly wings. "What you can't see here on the underside." He traced the edges with a finger. "Those spots are silver, not black. Silver!"

Rochelle frowned at me. "What?" She put her hands on her hips. "She doesn't look like Aphrodite to you?"

I opened my mouth to speak.

"How about Eve?" Big Al stepped back from the painting. "Would you feel better if we called her Eve? Garden of Eden was in Egypt. Brown-skinned, nappy-headed people in Egypt."

Rochelle said, "How can she be Aphrodite and Eve at the same time?"

Big Al rocked back on his heels. "'Cause she's an archetype."

"A what?"

"It's like. She's the mother of us all."

I looked at the painting. She had a hero's bold face, all cheekbones and chin, almost impersonal. The eyes were blistering. Her skin was dark, dark brown, and her Afro stood away from her head, almost ceremonial, like a crown. For a second, I thought of how, in church, they called Jesus's mother, *Queen* Mary, Mother of God; but I couldn't hold on to the thought. She was not anyone's mother that I knew. I glanced at Rochelle, but she wouldn't look at me. I said, "How come there's no snake? If she's Eve, shouldn't you have a snake or an apple instead of that butterfly?"

He shook his head. "Don't have to. You're the serpent. The *spec*tator. The *on*looker. You bring the knowledge, the corruption."

"The what?"

He nodded. "You heard me right."

"I'll have to think about that."

He laughed a soft laugh. "You go ahead."

21

MADEMOISELLE EUGÉNIE AND MIRIAM DID NOT arrive in a minute, as Big Al promised. They did not arrive in an hour. Instead, Miriam telephoned and explained they would be home late, after supper. They were at the house of a rich man, a famous musical composer, who they hoped would give money to Jean.

I said, "Is that why she came here, to Provincetown, to get money?"

Big Al nodded. "And to see Miriam. Miriam helps people—how would you put it, Shelle? She gets people on their way. Their journeys."

But Rochelle only shrugged, like she could care, and turned her back to Big Al. In this way, she sent her disdain, bouncing it, from him to me.

That night, Alphonse made blueberry pancakes for supper. The thing was, I couldn't eat. For some reason Rochelle was angry. All I'd said was: the Greek goddess of love. Big Al liked having pancakes for supper. Neither Rochelle nor me told him about the Big Breakfast, which we'd eaten a lifetime ago. Before Rochelle had gotten so angry. Every second now, I could feel the flat surface of my skin. At the kitchen table, Rochelle ate one pancake after another. I closed my eyes so as not to be sick. Honest to God, I was trembling. They say the skin is the largest organ of the human body. The heaviest. All my feelings were lodged in my throat. Well, maybe not all of them. I never thought of the skin as an organ like that. Rochelle didn't speak to me at supper. Didn't once look my way. All my feelings were lodged in my esophagus. I thought perhaps I could feel that place where the esophagus opened out, into the stomach, like a river dumping into a lake. Perhaps I could. I closed my eyes and pictured the terrible lake.

After supper, Big Al suggested, while we wait, that we three take a walk on the beach. I said yes immediately, which turned out to be a mistake: It gave Rochelle the opportunity to say no, which of course she took. If only I'd let her speak first! If only I'd waited to see what she had wanted to do! Big Al offered to drive me there, to a beach called Race Point. Now it was impossible to say no. He said it was the actual tip of the Cape, the one you saw on all the maps of the state.

When we got to his car—Big Al's was long and stately, cream-colored—not at all what you'd expect—I sort of panicked and ran back to ask Rochelle, to beg her to come. When I found her, she was in the kitchen, hunched over the phone. She didn't see me.

"Will you tell her I'm all right? When she gets in? Tell her Jean wanted me to come." She switched to her other ear. "Tell her not to worry. We'll be back first thing in the morning." Her voice cracked, rose. "I'm sixteen, she can't baby me all my life. Tell her Jean says that. Tell her Jean says she can't baby me forever!"

I backed out of the room. I'd more or less forgotten about the aunt, but, of course, Rochelle hadn't. Of course not. I mean, we'd borrowed her aunt's car without permission; the technical term for that was stealing. It made all the sense in the world that she would call home, explain the situation. At the same time, there was something in Rochelle's tone, some-thing desperate and pleading that I knew she wouldn't want me to hear.

I ran back to the car, to Big Al. It seemed like every second now I wanted to cry. As soon as I sat, Big Al shifted into reverse; the stick was on the tree, on the trunk of the stately steering wheel. As we drove through the empty town, it occurred to me—I kept one hand on the door handle, ready to jump out. It occurred to me he might.

Honest to God that town was lonesome! Big Al drove like an old person, leaning forward, peering out over the cream-colored steering wheel. As he drove, he talked about painting. I asked him why he always painted the same one.

He shrugged. "You'd think I'd know, but I don't. I start out trying to paint something else, and I always end up with her."

"How long have you been painting her?"

"Six years."

"Six *years*?"

He shook his head. "I know, I know."

"Is it like you're trying to get it right? Like you're not satis-fied, so you keep trying?"

He rubbed his face with his speckled hand. He rubbed his eyes. "It's more like, I'm exhausted. It's more like, she's wear-ing me out." He made that sound again deep in his throat, although this time it was not the sound of satisfaction.

I had the urge to ask him what was so wrong, so terrible, about having said the Greek goddess of love.

At Race Point, he stayed inside the parked car and read. I'd never been to the ocean at night. Now I saw I'd never been to the ocean at all: Carson Beach wasn't the ocean at all. From the water's edge, I could see the light in the car, Big Al's elaborate, lion's head bent over his book. The water was so loud, I could not hear myself think. I inched as close to the edge as I could. The water threw itself onto the beach and wet my clothes. I had always thought, before, that grief was simply sadness, simply missing someone. The stars were so bright they didn't move. Didn't twinkle, the way you always heard they did. I hadn't known then, with grief, there was no place to do the missing *from*. The shiny water threw itself again and again at my feet. I felt cold. The water and sky seemed one terrible, roaring thing. I could not hear myself weep.

Back at the house, Big Al suggested we take baths and a nap. I didn't think I could put my whole body into the bath, to feel the warm water press against my skin. But at the same time, I was funky. Funky from our drive to the Cape, from all that stopping. There's a kind of nasty stink you get when you're afraid. And I had been afraid all day.

Rochelle went first and, of course, she used up all the hot water. Now she went from room to room without looking at me. Not even out the corner of her eye. Was it so terrible, the thing I'd said? When it was my turn, I sat on the toilet and watched the bath filling up cold. It was one of those old-fashioned tubs with paws for feet. I went back and forth to the kitchen, boiling water.

When the bath was finally hot enough and full, I locked the door and took off all my clothes. I stood naked in front of the long mirror. Things were not impressively assembled, not well spaced out. I was too square-looking. For instance, there was not enough distance between my hips and my boobs. Plus, no real curve to speak of. It occurred to me: Maybe Rochelle wasn't so much mad, as disappointed. Disappointed with the way I was. Why wouldn't she be? My skin looked so white it was almost blue. Where it wasn't white, it was red, freckled, splotchy.

I climbed into the tub and smelled Rochelle's smell, which was still there. Of course, it made me horny again. To tell the truth, I didn't want to feel those feelings. Not now, when she was angry. I sank my whole body, my head under the water. All

I'd said was the Greek goddess of love. Was that so terrible? The horniness was practically against my will. It made me angry that she was angry. Honest to God it did.

But then it occurred to me: Maybe there was something else? Some mistake I'd made before, in the car? I raised my head out of the water. Touching her? Not touching her? It made me crazy, sick, to think I'd made a mistake like that. It made me hate myself. I'd give anything to try again, to do whatever it was she wanted. But just thinking that thought sent this flash of heat across my skin. I sat up, out of the water. I couldn't hold off, couldn't wait any longer. I pulled myself onto the ledge of the tub and opened my legs and put my fingers in and pictured her. I pictured Rochelle.

22

WHEN MADEMOISELLE EUGÉNIE FINALLY ARRIVED, it was way late, hours after Miriam had said, and I'd fallen asleep on the couch. Rochelle slept in one of the bedrooms. I had tried to wait up with Big Al; Rochelle had refused. He'd put the television on without sound, and we'd sat in the living room and watched the news. Rochelle had refused to be in the same room with me. Big Al said he liked to keep abreast of things, informed, but at the same time, he couldn't handle the actual things the television reporters talked about, world events. So we watched them move their mouths while Rochelle slept. As I drifted off, I remember thinking about Ma, wondering if, when I came home, she would really not let me back into the house, as, years before, she had not let my father.

At some point, Alphonse must have gone to bed himself, because when Mademoiselle Eugénie shook me awake, I was the only one in the living room.

"Ann," she said, "Ann. *Réveille-toi.*"

Her bouffant hairdo was gone. In its place, a Natural, only it didn't look natural, just wrong.

"Ann."

She looked grief-struck, old.

The thing was, people had other lives. Lives that didn't include you. You saw them in school or at work or what have you, and you thought about them in this one particular way, this one particular light. There was so much you couldn't imagine. Everything, really.

She settled onto the end of the couch. "I regret that we are not here when you arrive."

I sat up, kicked the blanket off my feet. I glanced at the new, short hair.

Frowning, she touched the fuzzy edge of her Natural.

Across from us, on the television, was the picture of those bright horizontal lines. What time was it?

She followed my eyes, then stood and shut off the television. Even without the sound, you could feel it pushing itself into the room. She said, "We must be going soon." She touched her long stem of a neck. "We must be taking the car."

"What car?"

"The car of Colleen Washington."

"Are you? Are those someone else's clothes?"

She looked down at too-big dungarees and a flannel work shirt. She laughed, but it was not a laugh that I recognized. "Colleen Washington called here. She is thinking that we must not remain long in Provincetown."

"Is Rochelle in trouble?"

She waved her hand dismissively. "Colleen Washington is thinking we must leave tonight. She is afraid the police have been learning my—how do you say?—my whereabouts."

"Where we going then?"

Mademoiselle Eugénie came back to the couch and sat; even in those borrowed clothes she looked regal, immaculate. Not American. Her spine was like a pole. She tilted her head, considering. "It is better, *je crois,* not to be telling you."

Like *I Spy!* These people—between her and the aunt—

every second it was *I Spy!* I wanted to wake Rochelle, I wanted
to tell her. I said, "Are we going to wake Rochelle?"

"*Pas encore.*"

"What are we waiting for?"

"It is better, *je crois,* that she is sleeping now."

"Rochelle's mad at me."

"*Comment?*"

I couldn't keep the words from falling out of my mouth.
"She's mad at me."

"*Mais, pourquoi?*"

"It's hard to explain." I lifted my arm, gestured vaguely at
Double Aphrodite. "I guess I said something about the paintings. I guess I said something about the Greek goddess of love."

Mademoiselle Eugénie nodded like she understood. "*Mais,
bien, oui.*" She sucked in air, a kind of reverse sigh. A gesture, a
sound that I'd heard her make before and that I understood was
French. Right then, I saw that there was still something, well,
between us. I don't mean *Romeo and Juliet,* the Montagues and
Capulets: I had been wrong when I'd imagined that before, that
night in Jamaica Plain. But there was still something. Some
familiarity or understanding. I couldn't say exactly what.

"Can I ask you something?"

"*Bien sûr.*"

"Why did you leave me that book?"

"*Ah, oui,* Rochelle did as I asked. *Très bien.*" She paused. "I
thought that you would be liking it."

"That's all?"

She shrugged. "I thought that you would be liking what he
has to say, *Monsieur Baldwin.*"

"The writer? That's funny. He reminded me of you. The
picture, I mean. I don't know why exactly." I frowned, trying
not to blush. "I mean, he's ugly and you're not." I couldn't stop.
"You're beautiful and he's not."

"*Monsieur Baldwin* spent several years in France, in Paris."

"Really? Did he like it there?"

"*Oui, et puis, non.* He went to jail in Paris. He was trying to escape his home, *les États-Unis.* He was trying to escape the prejudice here, in your country. But they were putting him in jail in Paris anyway."

I had never heard her use that word, prejudice. It sounded incredibly strange coming out of her mouth. Foreign. "Is he some kind of militant?"

She laughed, shaking her head. "*Non. Définitivement, non.* He is a writer. Writers are very rarely, how you said, militant? They are thinking too much about their own self. They are thinking always of their own feeling." She looked down at her hands. There was an expression on her face I couldn't read. "*Peut-être* you will be a writer one day." She puckered her lips. "The letters you wrote me, *elles étaient très bien faites,* very well done."

I frowned again. "Really?"

She looked up and nodded.

Then, suddenly, in my mind's eye, she was standing in front of our French class, explaining the sound of the French *u,* how it wasn't the same as the American *oo,* how it was an altogether different sound, although Americans always confused them. This was maybe a week after Halloween. She was wearing a reddish-brown dress with short sleeves, and I remember noticing how pointed her elbows were, how pointed and thin. No matter how many times she repeated the French sound, the class couldn't understand. Or wouldn't. She told us to pucker our mouths like we were going to kiss someone; she told us to whistle to get the sound right. But no one did. Later that same day, I saw her in the hallway: She was standing with her back to me, holding each of her pointed elbows in the palm of the opposite hand. Like a bird with its wings tucked in. I remember thinking she must be cold, in those short sleeves. I remember wanting to go up to her and say I understood that in order to learn a foreign language you had to be willing to move your mouth.

Now in Big Al's living room, she said, "Your writing, it will take you out of South Boston, *si tu veux.*"

Maybe you always loved the person or people who taught you to speak. Whoever they were. Your mother or your father, it didn't matter. Who taught you to express yourself. Whoever they were.

"*Monsieur Baldwin,* his writing took him out of Harlem. How do you say, the ghetto?"

Now there was something unfamiliar in her voice. Something disconcerting.

"One day, *si tu veux,* perhaps your writing will take you all the way to France!"

I bit my lip. Ma always said that flattery was a form of bullying. That people flattered you when they wanted you to do something for them.

"Of course, you must work hard. Is this even necessary to say? You must *travailler beaucoup. Beaucoup! Bien sûr.*"

More than anything, I wanted to believe what she was saying. I wanted to believe she thought I was talented, smart. But there was something, well, phony in her voice; her enthusiasm was trumped-up. Besides, it was one thing for me to say that I wanted to leave Southie. It was another thing for her to assume that I did. That irritated me. I tried to make my voice sound nonchalant. I said, "But I don't want to leave South Boston."

"*Non?*"

I shook my head.

"*Vraiment?* And here, I had the impression that you did."

I shrugged.

"You said, *je me souviens,* the day we were in the class together. The day of the *manifestation.* Do you remember that day? You said that you wanted to travel."

I stood up. I didn't know how to respond. I didn't want to

be angry at Mademoiselle Eugénie. "Rochelle says you're going underground."

Her eyelids fluttered.

"But why? I mean, you didn't do anything wrong!"

She pouted, tilting her head, and the pout turned into a frown. "After those boys set fire to my automobile, the police are very interested in me. They want one conversation, then another. The police—everywhere, *every*where—the police are speaking to each other. *Tu comprends?* It is better for me to be avoiding police stations altogether."

Suddenly I didn't want to go. I didn't want to get into that car. She was not who I thought she was! I whispered, "What did you do?"

"*Pardon?*"

"What crime did you commit?"

She shook her head. "*Ce n'était pas un crime.*"

"What then?"

She paused. She ironed an imaginary wrinkle from the front of her borrowed shirt. Without looking up, she went into this long explanation about the government in France and how it was closing its doors to immigrants from Africa, its former colonies, what she called the Maghreb. The explanation was so long, so detailed, I found myself drifting off, in that way I have. Drifting off when I should have been paying the most attention. Tunisia, Algeria, Morocco. She said she was part of a group that protested the government's policy.

"But you're not from there?" I said.

She looked up. "*Non. Je viens d'Afrique,* but not the Maghreb."

"I don't understand," I said.

"That does not surprise me."

"Do you think? I mean, will you ever come to Southie again?"

She raised her shoulders up, in a delicate shrug, like she

didn't know, like who could know the answer to such a difficult question, when I knew that she did. She knew! Of course she did. She would never set foot in Southie for as long as she lived. Why should she?

Then I remembered the *arrondissements.* Out of nowhere. I remember the left bank and the right. I remembered Mademoiselle Kit Kelly and how exasperated she'd been when I'd gotten them confused. She'd even shown us her little book, *Le plan de Paris.* How stupid she was! I pictured her blank freckled face. The map of Ireland, the map of France. How stupid she'd been to even try to teach us French!

I crossed to the other side of the room. Mademoiselle Eugénie was still on the couch, still holding her shoulders up, in that ridiculous shrug. On the wall behind her was Big Al's butterfly Aphrodite. An archetype—how ridiculous was that! Either you were Eve or Queen Mary, Mother of God, or the Greek goddess of love. You couldn't be all three of them at once. You could not! The truth was, I'd never leave fucking Southie my whole useless life, no matter how far I went.

Now for the first time since I'd met her, Mademoiselle Eugénie seemed ugly to me.

"*Ann,*" she said, "there is something that I am needing you to do."

More than anything, I hated when my mother was right.

"A favor. *En français,* we say, *une grâce.*"

"A grace?"

"*Oui, une grâce.*"

23

I AM TEMPTED TO SAY THAT ALL ALONG I HAD KNOWN what it was that Mademoiselle Eugénie wanted from me. The favor, the grace. From that night in Jamaica Plain, all along I had known. It is true that she more or less asked me then. She looked at me, after telling us what had happened—those boys setting fire to her car—she looked at me—her penciled-on eyebrows were gone—and said, "Do you remember, *Ann*, the boy with the flag?"

But that would not be entirely correct. Entirely honest. It would be more honest to say that I had known it once and then forgot. *Forgot* is a strange word; it's as if the forgetting happens *to you* instead of you being the one who does it. There was a way Mademoiselle Eugénie's absence allowed me to forget. Her absence from school let me think about her exactly how I wanted to: the bouffant hairdo; the tight, bright, French clothes. In my mind's eye I pictured her, standing in the hallway, a vivid bird—an oasis of pleasure!—and I forgot about what she'd asked me that night in Jamaica Plain. It was the easiest thing in the world to forget.

Now in Provincetown, she asked again, for the second time, but more directly. She wanted me to tell them the name of the boy who'd set fire to her car. They—her *I Spy* friends from those *I Spy* meetings—had decided the police would never find him. Mademoiselle Eugénie had already guessed, since South Boston was such a small town, that I would know the name of the boy who, during the *manifestation* which we had watched, had stood on the parked car and waived the American flag. Who was also the boy—she told me now—tall, *maigre*, the leader—who'd sprinkled gasoline like he was watering plants—who'd held her arm and made her look, *Regarde, regarde*: He was also the boy who'd set fire to her car.

The favor was for me to be a Benedict Arnold. Me, Ann Ahern, a girl from South Boston! But where was the grace in that, I wanted to know? Where was the grace in telling on someone?

Especially someone you knew.

Because of course it was someone I knew. South Boston *was* such a small town. It was stupid Mike McGuire and his elephant balls. At the time, I hadn't let myself say the words—his stupid name—out loud. I hadn't even permitted myself to say it silently, secretly. Why would I? Why on earth would I? It was stupid Mike McGuire who, according to Flynn, broke the second commandment whenever he came.

Jesus, Flynn!

Christ, Flynn!

Mother of God, Flynn!

That is, according to my ex-best friend, Patty Flynn.

I told Mademoiselle Eugénie no way. No *way*.

She acted surprised, her soft mouth suddenly tight. Surprised and disappointed. She shook her head. *"C'est dommage, dommage*. Too bad." She sighed that French sigh, breathing in instead of out. "Perhaps you will change your mind? Perhaps you will think about it for a little while?"

I told her not in a million years.

24

IN MY NEXT-TO-LAST SESSION WITH DR. MCGRAUGH (the state paid for a total of seventeen), he said that for the rest of my life I would have to accept that I had, what he termed, poor impulse control. In other words, when I got pissed, I did what I wanted to do. Or, at least, it was hard for me not to. During that session, he gave me a rubber band to wear. He actually put it on my wrist. He said whenever I got the impulse to burn something, to set a fire, I should flick the rubber band. It was a way of pinching myself. Of reminding me who and where I was: Ann Ahern, a girl from South Boston, a girl with poor impulse control. But to tell the truth, when I looked around, I had to ask myself, who didn't? Who didn't have a short fuse? What I did—setting fires—might have been more severe, more noticeable than what Ma and Flynn did— which was basically fuck guys—lots and lots of guys—but was it really so much worse? Okay, okay, there was a degree of— Dr. McGraugh again—*antisocial* sentiment in what I did, but at least I sent my anger out, into the world. Instead of drawing it toward me.

Which was the difference, if you thought about, between guys and girls. And which was why I wasn't considered exactly normal, from a guy-girl point of view. Maybe, come to think of it, maybe I was a lezzie not so much because I liked girls, but because I sent my anger out, into the world, into the swirling galaxy.

I wore the rubber band for a long time, a year maybe. At first Ma checked to make sure I was wearing it whenever I left the house. I remember the bite of the pinch. I remember snapping it as hard as I could. After a while, I did it just to feel the sting; the skin on the inside of my wrist got raw, rubbed-away. I was getting closer and closer to the blue vein. At some point, I can't remember when, the rubber band broke. That was when I took to carrying matches wherever I went. In a funny way, it served the same purpose. Whenever I felt the desire to burn something, I'd finger the clean, square edge of the match-book cover; I'd press its hard pointy corners under my finger-nails. At the same time, touching those matches did something else as well. I'd get this surge of adrenaline. I'd get the flush of pleasure I got when I actually burned something. The famous release about which Dr. McGraugh had told Ma. After, when I brought my fingers to my mouth, I tasted sulphur.

Now in that small, gray-shingled house in Provincetown, I felt for the matches in my pocket. I was pissed off. I was unbe-lievably, incredibly angry. All this time I had thought that Mademoiselle Eugénie was interested in me. Me, in particular! I had thought she wanted to be friends. But instead, she wanted me to be a traitor, a coward. She wanted me to turn over some poor Southie kid so her *I Spy* friends could do what-ever they wanted! I didn't think I'd ever been so angry in all my life. At the same time, I had to control myself. Contain myself. The fury. I was far from home. Miles and miles from South Boston. I had to get in that car and drive off the Cape with Mademoiselle Eugénie. I had to act like everything was okay, normal; like she hadn't asked me to be a Benedict Arnold. And I had to convince Rochelle. Somehow, I had to convince Rochelle that Mademoiselle Eugénie was definitely not who she thought she was.

I mean, sure, Rochelle knew she was going underground, knew she was some kind of militant. But Rochelle didn't know she had asked me to be a coward, a rat. In my world, telling on someone—especially someone you knew—was pretty much the worst thing you could do. I mean, sure, everyone was glad that Nixon was gone, but no one could stomach that guy with the glasses, what was his name? John Dean. He had a weasel's face. I was sure it was the same where Rochelle lived. Kids my age pretty much lived by the same codes wherever you went, it didn't matter. Roxbury or Southie or Jamaica Plain. I was pretty certain it was the same with Rochelle. Black or White, it didn't matter. Almost 100 percent certain. No matter what, she wouldn't want me to be a Benedict Arnold, a John Dean. I mean, in the end, how could she love a weasel? I didn't think that she could.

Still, I had to get through the rest of the night. I had to compose myself for the drive off the Cape. One of the few useful things I actually learned from Dr. McGraugh was to break things down. He said that whenever I felt overwhelmed—by my anger or by feelings of any kind—I should break things down into their consecutive parts, one thing, then the next. One step at a time, he actually said, smiling stupidly. I hated those kinds of expressions, but I was desperate. I was desperate enough to take things step-by-step.

The next step was counting the money. Now we were in the kitchen, at the rickety supper table. Except Miriam didn't call it money, she called it bread, dough. Everything about that kitchen was small, cramped; under the table, our knees bumped. Was it two in the morning? Three? Our nervous knees kept knocking each other. Because of the hour, because Aunt Colleen had insisted we leave tonight—it was dangerous to stay, she'd said, the pigs would come—everything had a feverish quality. Miriam kept licking her thumb, applying the wet pad to the corner of the bills.

Miriam was White. Big Al's wife. I must have looked surprised. She was blonde, petite. When she saw the look on my face, she laughed. You must be *Ann Ahern*. Miriam's laugh was like a little dog's bark. *Hip, hip, hip!* Between making stacks of tens, stacks of twenties, she told us what had happened at the house of the famous musical composer.

"He couldn't keep his fucking eyes off Jean. I'd always heard he was a faggot, but I guess not. He brought us over to the piano, made Jean sit next to him on the bench while he played song after song from that pretentious musical of his. What's it called? When he finished he said, 'I'd really like to ball you.'" *Hip, hip, hip!* "Just like that. Fucking bourgeois bastard."

Rochelle sat at my elbow. She'd been woken up by Miriam, and her face still had creases from the sheets, the pillow. Otherwise, she was wide awake. Otherwise, she was incredibly excited. When she'd sat, she'd actually smiled at me. She was so excited, it seemed, she'd forgotten about the Greek goddess of love. She sat next to me and stared across the table at Mademoiselle Eugénie.

I wanted to smooth the creases on her long, dark face. I wanted to tell her Mademoiselle Eugénie was not who she thought she was. At the same time, I was incredibly relieved that she wasn't angry anymore.

"How much bread he give you?" Big Al stood behind his wife and squeezed her shoulders.

Miriam shook her head, her thin lips still counting the money.

I was so relieved, I felt this actual release in my neck. This click and release. I swiveled my head as far as it would go in each direction.

When she finished counting, Miriam slapped the table.

"Fucking liberal cheapskate! Doesn't he realize how much it costs to go underground these days?"

"Whoa, baby, whoa." Big Al patted her shoulders.

Rochelle reached into her pocket and tossed the rest of our cash onto the table.

Mademoiselle Eugénie shook her head in protest.

Rochelle shrugged, sheepish. "It's my aunt's bread anyway."

Miriam scooped up the money, then righted a stack that had spilled. I had never seen so much cash before. So much bread. So much dough. Miriam glanced at Mademoiselle Eugénie. "Colleen says she doesn't want Rochelle in the car with you and Ann. She wants Big Al to take her home." Miriam cut the two stacks in half, then folded the bills over and cinched each half around with a fat paper clip. "In case you get stopped. Colleen doesn't want her niece to risk any encounter with the pigs."

Rochelle stood up so fast she knocked over her chair. "Don't talk like I'm not here! Like it's not my decision!"

Miriam handed the wads of money to Mademoiselle Eugénie. "The drop-off is in Plymouth. There'll be a car waiting for you in the parking lot of the Holiday Inn." Then to Rochelle, without even looking at her: "You think I'm going against your aunt, you're dreaming."

Now I stood. More than anything I wanted Rochelle and me to be on the same side. A team. "I think Rochelle should come. Definitely. I mean, it's her aunt's car and everything."

Miriam just laughed.

But Rochelle looked at me and smiled. To tell the truth, it was the first time all night that she really took me in. That she recognized me. More than anything I wanted her to understand that I had to live—even if Ma threw me out—I had to live in South Boston, didn't I? I thought for sure she'd understand. Besides, I didn't want to be alone in the car with Mademoiselle Eugénie. Now that I knew what she wanted from me.

I smiled back at Rochelle to show my gratitude, then turned to Miriam and said, "Rochelle drives better than me. Way better. I mean, I can't even drive standard."

Miriam frowned. "Is that true?"

Now everyone looked at me. There was Rochelle's long, hopeful face; there was Mademoiselle Eugénie's gently puckered mouth. Everything she did, every gesture and expression, seemed phony, pretend. Big Al's face was warm, concerned, absolutely without desire or opinion. You could tell he wouldn't take a position on anything. He looked like he wanted to get back to his painting, to exhausting Double Aphrodite and her identical friends. Next to him, Miriam flicked her head left then right, watching, waiting for someone to answer her question. She didn't let anything by her. It was a commitment she'd made years ago. Her hair was white, white blonde and ironed flat except for some pieces that crinkled up around her temples. I thought probably Double Aphrodite was less exhausting than Miriam.

Mademoiselle Eugénie cleared her throat. Politely, delicately. She looked down at her hands, pushing back the cuffs of her borrowed sleeves. There were the silver bracelets she'd worn in class! She was in disguise, she was traveling incog— could you say that a Black person was traveling incog-Negro? I didn't know the answer to that; I'd have to ask. I'd have to ask Rochelle when we were on the road. When we had—I was hoping we were going to have a moment of privacy, just the two of us, together, on the road. There was so much that I wanted to tell her. It was like we'd been separated for a long time; it was like we were long-lost lovers finally reunited. I wanted to tell her about everything she'd missed, about the drive to the beach, to Race Point; how Big Al had stayed in the car; how the water and the sky had been one terrible, roaring thing; how the stars didn't twinkle the way you always heard they did; about the grief I'd felt. I wanted to tell her about later, in the tub, touching myself. And I wanted to ask her why, hours and hours before, when we'd been alone together in the car, why she hadn't let me touch her. More than anything, I wanted to ask her that.

But now, Mademoiselle Eugénie dropped her hands, and those silver bracelets jangled lightly, musically, at her hips. She looked up. "Do not be worrying," she said. "I will be taking the responsibility. Tomorrow, I will be talking with Colleen Washington." She addressed Miriam, but her gaze seemed far away, unfocused. "I will explain everything. I am sure it will be a good experience, *tu vois,* a kind of opportunity, for Rochelle. The drive to Plymouth. Why should Ann Ahern benefit when Rochelle Washington does not? The drop-off. *Tu comprends?* When I was her age. A girl, she had to prove herself. She had to prove that she was, *on disait,* willing and worthy. I think this will be an excellent opportunity for Rochelle. Life presents each of us with different—" and here she paused and looked intently at Rochelle, her eyes once again sharp, in focus; her gaze, her whole Mademoiselle self, once again utterly, fantastically present: "When I was a girl, *on disait,* willing and worthy."

PART FIVE

Beyond Beyond

25

THAT FIRST YEAR OF BUSING, PRACTICALLY THE ONLY militant group you heard about was the Symbionese Liberation Army, which had captured Patty Hearst. At first, she was against them. On cassette tapes they sent to the newspaper, she begged for her life: *Daddy, please do everything they tell you.* But after a while, after her father had paid to airlift fresh bananas into poor sections of California, she joined up, she enlisted in the SLA. She was fighting her family then. On one of the final tapes, she called her father a capitalist pig. She said that from now on, they should call her Tania, because Patty was dead.

Ma says the old Irish believe that before someone dies a banshee sits under the window of the house and wails. You can't see the banshee; she's a kind of fairy, not a nice one; they're not all nice, for Christ's sake; they're not all freaking leprechauns, but you can hear her awful-sounding wails. In the car, as we drove off the Cape, I kept thinking: Mademoiselle Eugénie is dead! The Mademoiselle I knew. Dead. *Dead.* In the car, as we drove, I kept listening for the banshee.

What I heard instead was my own panic, my own terror. I

was terrified I was going to lose Rochelle to Mademoiselle Eugénie. To whatever phony, pretend, *I Spy* thing that she was offering.

Rochelle was in the backseat. Of course, I drove. I drove and drove on the exact same road, Route 6. Of course, I was horny again. Only now, *horny* was the wrong word, was insufficient. It didn't capture all of how I felt. I felt hysterical. Like an animal. Like weeping. We were in reverse, going back exactly the way we'd come, but you'd never know it. I mean, Rochelle didn't even acknowledge the Monopoly-sized motel or the empty parking lot where we'd stopped just *hours* before. I kept trying to catch her eye, to get her attention. Instead, the two of them talked and talked. I swear they talked like I wasn't even in the car.

Rochelle crouched on the awkward hump, her head bobbing between me and Mademoiselle Eugénie. "Colleen says, during Civil Rights, all of America knew we were right. You can see it in the pictures—those sour White faces—even the piggy pigs knew." She gripped and regripped the back of our seats. "Their days were numbered. Their time was passing. The more they realized it, the more evil they got." She shook her head. "But we've lost that.

"The first time I climbed on one of those buses to Southie, I thought, all right, now I'm a part of something. All right, now it's my turn! There was this feeling of, you know," she looked at Mademoiselle Eugénie, "connection. All the Black folks who'd gone before you."

Mademoiselle Eugénie nodded.

"But also a feeling of, of righteousness! When those White parents started throwing rocks at the buses—not just my bus, but fourth graders! Second graders! It felt like I was at—what did Colleen say?—the moral center of the universe." Rochelle's dark brown face was red, glowing.

Mademoiselle Eugénie shifted in her seat, tucking a long

leg beneath her, in order to face Rochelle. *"Oui, oui,"* she said.
"Oui, oui."

Rochelle frowned. "But for some reason, it didn't last."
Shook her head. "That recognition. People got bored with
desegregation, impatient. Protest after protest, those Southie
mothers down on their knees praying. People lost interest. I'm
talking about White people in the suburbs. I'm telling you,
White people are tired of feeling bad about themselves. They're
through with it."

I stared out the windshield at the narrow, empty road, at
the faint white and yellow lines passing beneath the car. Hear-
ing Rochelle talk this way gave me the flattest feeling in the
world. The emptiest. It occurred to me that no one in the
entire universe knew where I was. I mean, no one in my family. No one in the whole swirling galaxy. We passed signs for
Mashpee, Sandwich.

"What I'm saying is, used to be Black people who were
praying. But now it's those White ladies saying their Hail
Marys! How you gonna ask God to keep your children away
from Black folks?" She gripped our headrests so hard, she was
practically pulling herself into the front seat. "Can someone
explain that to me?"

Mademoiselle Eugénie shook her head.

"How does a prayer like that *sound*?" Rochelle paused,
grunted. A wave of feeling passed over her face. "I want to be
part of something, you know, larger and all. But most days, it
feels like I'm a part of nothing. Like everything's standing
still."

"What you are noticing is, the moment for desegregation,
it is over. Past." Mademoiselle Eugénie paused, sucking in her
breath. "It is time for something else, another strategy."

"Like what?"

And I thought to myself: No, no, no!

"Where I am going there are many Black people." She

nodded. "Many." She seemed to be considering something. "Do you know the expression, *on disait en anglais,* the Black belt?"

"I've heard my aunt—" Rochelle stopped, shrugged. "Not really."

"It is a part of *les États-Unis.* States where *nous sommes* the majority. Mississippi, Louisiana, Alabama, Georgia, South Carolina."

"You're going *South?* South!" I was practically shouting. "That's the stupidest thing I've ever heard! They *hate* Blacks in the South!"

Rochelle snorted. "Not like Boston, huh, where you love us to death?"

"You know what I mean!" I was desperate, flailing.

Mademoiselle Eugénie shifted another inch in her seat. I didn't think it was possible for her to be ignoring me anymore than she already was. "*Nous sommes,* there are more of us in the South. *Tu vois?* That is to say, it is easier to organize."

Rochelle said quietly, "Organize what?"

Mademoiselle Eugénie frowned, then she pursed her lips, but the lips broke into a smile. It seemed almost against her will, the smile; now you could see every one of her straight, white teeth. Now she was beautiful again. "That is for us to decide, *non?*"

Rochelle raised her eyebrows.

No, no, no! I wanted to scream, to shout. Inside, I was wailing. Keening. I didn't know grief made you crazy like this, unhinged. A banshee. I mean, let's just say I decided to do what she'd asked, Mademoiselle Eugénie, her impossible favor, her impossible grace. It was one thing for me to lose my family, my ex-best friend, my entire freaking neighborhood; but it was another to lose all that and then lose Rochelle! I mean, how was I supposed to live? It was too much. Too much to have come this far, to have traveled this distance, only to be left

behind. I couldn't bear it. Now I hated Mademoiselle Eugénie.
Honest to God, I hated her more than anything.

I looked into the rearview mirror. I was trying to catch
Rochelle's eye. But she was sitting too far forward. I glanced
sideways at her. For a second, I took my eyes off the road and
said—finally, at long fucking last—I said: "She's not who you
think she is."

Rochelle turned, blinked. "Say again?"

Mademoiselle Eugénie sat back. She was surprised; I could
tell by the way she moved that I had surprised her. She tucked
herself against the passenger door and crossed her arms.

"Mademoiselle Eugénie asked me to be a Benedict Arnold."

Rochelle said, "What are you talking about?"

"She wants—" I glanced in the corner. Mademoiselle Eugénie looked at me with this unbelievably blank face. What you
might call impassive. Suddenly, I remembered how, when I
used to imagine her reading my letters, she'd gotten this blank
face. In my mind's eye, she'd lost the almond eyes, the painted-
on eyebrows, and the gently puckered mouth; and it had
scared me, that blank Black face. But now here it was, in real
life. I don't mean to suggest that her features were gone, erased;
it was that now I understood every expression she used was
fake. As she sat there, tucked against the passenger door, staring at me cold, impassive, I realized that now *Mademoiselle
Eugénie* was the wrong name for her; now *Jean* was better,
more accurate, more precise. Like *Tania*. I said to Rochelle,
"Jean wants me to tell her the name of that boy."

"What boy?" Rochelle's head whipped around. "What are
you talking about!"

We were both of us shouting.

"The boy—the leader—the one who set fire to her car!"

Rochelle sputtered. "You know!" She sucked in air like she
couldn't breathe, like she'd had the wind knocked out of her.
"The name of that boy!"

And so I turned to face her. I had to explain. I mean, everything that had happened since we'd left Jamaica Plain. I had to explain because even though we'd been traveling together, the two of us, a pair, somehow we'd had different, well, experiences. Her face still had the shadow of a crease from her sheets, her pillow. I actually took one hand off the wheel and reached out to smooth her cheek. And right then I saw that her face was melancholy, not horsey. I had been wrong before when I'd thought that she looked horsey; her face was full of feeling; that's why she seemed like an old soul; that's why she was so beautiful, although not in a typical, not in a girlish way: Always, always her face was full of intense expectancy.

But now, in her eyes, there was something else, something new. In the soft brown part. The part just above the white crescent, which was soft and wet, the rich, mixed color of pennies. Now there was terror. Now there was disgust. Rochelle Washington looked at me with terrified disgust.

Which was when the front tire on the passenger side slipped off the road. Just an inch or so. The tire slid onto the shoulder, which, on Route 6, is pretty much nothing but sand. We skidded. Immediately I took my foot off the accelerator, and the car slowed, but we continued to skid, and I had to yank the wheel to get us off the shoulder, off the sand. I pulled too hard, too sharply; now we were crossing the yellow line. We were the only car on the road, the only car for miles, but still, it was awful to be on the wrong side. I shifted down, down, into third, then second. But when I yanked the wheel again, in the opposite direction, to compensate for my first mistake, we skidded off the road, onto the shoulder, and beyond.

26

Beyond was a small, steep ditch that turned up just as steeply, just as suddenly, onto an embankment. The car came to an abrupt stop halfway up the incline. No one was badly hurt. The car just sat there steaming. I mean, we all were hurt a little bit, all of us thrown suddenly forward, Rochelle the farthest, into the windshield. Evidently she'd put her hands out to protect herself. Her wrists were cut from the windshield glass, cut and bleeding. So was her forehead. I hit the steering wheel; my chest and chin got slammed by the Duster's red steering wheel. Instantly, a sharp pain blossomed in my jaw. I tasted blood. And Mademoiselle Eugénie, who'd been sitting sideways, was thrown into the foot well of the passenger seat. She must have hit the side of her head on the glove compartment, because there was blood on her cheek, her temple. We were all three bruised and bleeding and definitely shook up, but no one, no one was seriously hurt.

It took us a few minutes to realize this, though. It took us a few minutes to stumble out the passenger door. My door was stuck. The driver's window had broken; the door looked somewhat crushed on its frame, and I couldn't open it. Mademoiselle Eugénie kicked open her door, she kicked with both feet—a gesture I never would have pictured her making—and climbed out. Because of the steep pitch of the embankment, and because of the sideways position in which the car had stopped, the passenger door was above us. In other words, when Mademoiselle Eugénie—Jean—kicked, she kicked up. The door kept falling shut. She kicked once, twice, three times, eventually holding it ajar with one foot.

Rochelle, who'd been tossed forward, into the windshield and then, somehow, tossed back, crawled off the hump and pretty much dragged herself out, onto the ground by the passenger door. I edged myself, an inch at a time, toward the opening; I was covered in glass. Finally I sat with my feet out the door. I stared at the ground, which was part dirt, part sand, part yellowed winter grass. Snowless. My position was awkward, hips and butt below knees and ankles, like an astronaut in a capsule. I watched Rochelle crawl, then stagger away from the door, and stand.

Mademoiselle Eugénie said *merde,* which, if you didn't already know, was a French swear word. She crouched by the front of the car, one hand on the steaming hood, one pressed against her bleeding temple. "Everyone is all right? *Mes filles?*" She straightened herself. *"Vous êtes blessés?"*

Rochelle looked at me. "You okay?"

My tongue throbbed.

She gestured with her chin. "There's a lot. There's blood. You lose any teeth?"

I felt gingerly along the bottom row. When I shook my head, the pain flowered again. My tongue felt heavy in my mouth. I reached up to cradle my cheek.

The gash on Rochelle's forehead was bleeding, and the blood ran down the center of her face, alongside her broad nose. Sighing, she wiped the blood with the sleeve of her sweatshirt. "Can't believe you know the name of that boy." Her voice was flat, matter of fact, defeated.

I shrugged carefully, carefully: The pain took every opportunity.

Mademoiselle Eugénie said, "We do not have much time.
Before the police will be arriving."

Rochelle said, "Who is it?"

But I shook my head. "You really?" My tongue was thick,
unaccustomed. "Want that?"

She frowned.

"For me to be? Benedict Arnold. John Dean."

"John who?"

"Watergate guy."

"Right, right." She nodded. It was dark by the side of the
road, no streetlights, but the moon was just bright enough so
that we could see. She glanced over her shoulder, into the
woods I was facing. Those woods were sparse, hardly woods at
all, but now they looked incredibly dark. She turned back to
me: "What about my aunt's car?"

I tried to shake my head without moving. "No way."

"Colleen's gonna break me in half."

I waited. I tried to get a hold of my useless tongue. I must've
bitten it when we crashed, really bitten it; which explained the
blood, the awkward slowness. Finally, I said, "What's it matter?
If Jean's going. Leaving. What's the difference who?"

Rochelle stepped back to the car. "You mean that? What's
the difference?"

The pain in my jaw was like those speeded-up flowers that
blossomed again and again.

"Are you simple?" She glanced at Mademoiselle Eugénie,
who was still resting against the hood. "Is she simple?"

Mademoiselle Eugénie shrugged then frowned; she kept
pushing her short Natural away from her bleeding temple.

Rochelle leaned her forearms against the frame of the
passenger door and looked down at me. "The difference is
because *I* have to go to school there, fool. *I* have to go to school

and sit in the same rooms and breathe the same air as those murderous White boys." She shook her head. "What is it with you people? Here you are, half crazy about me, half out-your-mind, and you don't even know why it's important to tell us the name of that boy." Shook it again. "What's wrong with you?"

"Don't say that."

"Say what?"

"Say *half*."

She stepped back and dropped her hands. "Dang! See there? That's exactly what I'm talking about."

For several minutes, no one spoke. We three listened to the noiseless air: no cars, no breeze, no busy animals. I watched the blood from Rochelle's wrists dribble down her long fingers. The blood dried the same color as her skin. I hated that she'd said *us—tell us the name of that boy*. Her arms hung like rope beside her body, her torso. She was long-waisted and long-legged; most people were one or the other, but she was both. Her waist was straight up and down. From this distance—we were only a couple of feet apart—I could smell her Black smell. I could smell the iron smell of the blood. Hers and mine. I wanted to lift her sweatshirt up and see the Black belly. Even though my jaw hurt. Even though my tongue throbbed. The thing about horniness was—I was just learning this—you couldn't simply shut it off. (The problem with English was either the words were too barren, too street—*horniness*—or too corny, inflated—*desire*. I wanted a regular way to speak: honest, not flowery, not street. I wondered about the words in French.) You couldn't shut the feeling off even when the pain in your mouth was unbelievably sharp. I wanted to lean forward and taste her Black belly with my bleeding tongue. I wanted her to say, *I'm half crazy about you too, Ann Ahern*. Or maybe, *I'm out-my-mind myself*. But she didn't. Wouldn't. It was not her way, her style: She held herself back. I knew that. But still, I wondered. I wondered if, during all this time, the two of us traveling together, on the road, if she hadn't been, even for a minute or two, in love with me? For a second.

But just having to ask—already I knew what the answer was. Which seemed terribly, terribly unfair—questions shouldn't answer themselves. If you loved someone, if you told them, or showed them, you deserved an answer. Didn't you? I shook my head against the unfairness. Now my tongue was numb. You deserved the grace of a response. Again and again I shook my head, until Rochelle said, "What?"

But before I could answer, before I could even try to get a hold of my tongue, there was the sound of a car approaching, and we all three heard it and looked down the embankment toward the road.

There were the headlights, gauzy in the night fog. The tires whirring against Route 6. My panic was like a knife peeling back skin. The car grew big, bigger. No blue police light, but suddenly, high beams, illuminating the embankment, our crooked car, our frozen limbs. Another sudden rush and the car was upon us, was passing—what exact color—yellow? tan? We watched it pull over and slow to a stop a few hundred yards ahead. Now its flashers came on, red, fitful, and a White man climbed out the driver's door.

What do you do in moments like these? You hold your breath. You count to ten. Make corny bargains. I told myself everything would be all right if I could count all the way to twenty. The man walked in the trail of flashing light. I told God I would do anything He wanted—give up girls, candy, not believing in Him—if only the White man coming toward us liked Black people. Or, at least, didn't dislike them in an aggressive, in a vengeful way. The man wore a three-piece suit, had a clipped beard. I made it to twenty. Now Mademoiselle Eugénie started down the embankment, ginger, determined; she slid carefully, her weight back on her heels, one hand pressing against her temple, one hand held out for balance.

27

ONCE, WHEN I WAS A KID, THE POLICE CAME TO OUR house. A neighbor, one of Ma's enemies, had reported her to child welfare for staying out all night at a party and leaving us unsupervised. I had taken care of Timmy, who was about ten months. He was a good baby, easier than the twins; I remember I put some cereal in his bottle and he slept through most of the night. I was ten, Hap was twelve, the twins, eight apiece. Plenty old, but they could have arrested Ma on a morals charge or for neglect, if they'd wanted to. It was purely a question of what they wanted; it always was with the police. Everybody in my neighborhood knew that.

I was holding Timmy when I answered the door. Ma was in the shower, she'd just gotten home. The cops were locals, guys we knew; one was a terrible drunk named Duffy, the other was young, I can't remember his name now, a gambler who lost money regularly at the racetrack in East Boston. The young cop drove Duffy home in the squad car every day, half the neighborhood watching as he carried his drunk partner up the steps. After they came inside, I made the gambler hold Timmy while I went for Ma. I remember the feeling of dread, the tightening in my chest. She told me to fix them tea and toast.

When the cops asked, I said I was thirteen. I held Timmy in one arm, poured hot water into their cups with the other. As a kid, we'd invented a game called Mean Mothers; I'd always been good, always played a mother; I was tall for my age. In the next room, the twins were watching cartoons. The music revved like an engine, then stopped. From the kitchen, I pictured the coyote dropping, one part of his body falling ahead of the rest. Hap was already out. The cops balanced their hats on their knees and ate their toast.

When Ma came down from her shower, they stood. She had dressed for work—a part-time operator for the phone company, then—which meant high heels and slacks and a clingy blouse—though her shift wasn't till that night. Her orange hair was still wet. The party she'd stayed so long at had been for her; she'd just turned twenty-nine. She lit a cigarette and put on her operator voice: How can I help you gentlemen? She sounded official, as if they were working together to solve some telephone crime. Two weeks later, Ma stayed out all night with the young gambler.

In this way, Mademoiselle Eugénie reminded me of Ma: She was hard not to admire. Even if you disagreed with her. Even if you were opposed to the things she said, what she stood for, her unbelievable, freaking selfishness: She was hard not to admire a little bit. Because of her moxie. Her willingness. Mademoiselle Eugénie was the first to reach the foot of the embankment. The first to reach the sandy shoulder. She nodded to the approaching White man, then turned and reached a hand out—protective, regal—toward Rochelle and me. But the thing was, in the end, with Ma, your admiration always worked against you; in the end, it always did.

Turned out, the man wasn't vengeful. Wasn't the police. He was just a lawyer, going to work in Boston. He was concerned about the blood, our bruises. Should he take us to the hospital? We three shook our heads almost in unison. A lawyer and

Good Samaritan. To tell the truth, I couldn't quite get over my terror. My sense of exposure. We stood on the shoulder, blinking, unspeaking. He said it was possible all three of us were in shock.

The man explained that he commuted from his house in Chatham, a two-hour drive, but worth the effort. In the early morning, there were never any cars on the road. When he said this, he looked over at our broken car, no longer steaming, on the embankment. He glanced at his watch, rubbed his neat beard with the back of his hand. It was five in the morning. The sky was brightening, a dark green, behind him. We stood shivering, listening to him tell his story. He'd been a hippie then a baker. When he turned forty he gave up and went to law school. His wife made jewelry. I realized this was his way of saying: I won't harm you. He was a real-life Good Samaritan.

I thought probably we were in shock, but not in the way that he meant.

When we got to his car—small, foreign, yellow; he'd had it years before the energy crisis—he pulled down the driver's seat, and we all climbed in the back.

He laughed an embarrassed laugh. "Of course, you can— what are your names? Miss? You're welcome to sit up front." He gestured with an open palm, his eyes on Mademoiselle Eugénie. She shook her head.

He coughed. "Girls?" He looked at me.

I shrugged. Rochelle, the first to climb in, stared out the window.

Now he was truly uncomfortable. "I'll just drop you off, then, how's that? In Bourne. At the pancake house. It's the only thing open. You can call the police from there."

There was a stiffening—could he feel it?—the molecules in the backseat stuttering to a halt.

He felt it. He glanced in the rearview mirror. "The police will call a tow truck."

Mademoiselle Eugénie nodded. She sat between Rochelle and me, hands on her knees.

"It's just, it's cheaper that way. If you call the tow yourself, you have to pay. But if the police call, it's the state's dime."

It occurred to me that the less we spoke, the more strange we seemed. The more we stood out.

When he eased the car back onto Route 6, he said, "Where you girls coming from? Where on the Cape?"

I looked at Mademoiselle Eugénie. Probably she didn't want him to hear her speak. If someone asked, if the police interviewed him later, her accent would be the thing he'd remember. That and her dark dark skin. I said, "The pancake house will be fine."

We drove in awkward silence under the Sagamore Bridge, along the twinkling canal. Now there were cars on the road; the sky turned lavender. Mademoiselle Eugénie craned her neck, watching out the windows. The man kept glancing at us. Rochelle was so still, so quiet, it was like she wasn't even in the car. I had the urge to tell her that I understood—for the first time—I understood what it felt like to be afraid in this particular way.

The Good Samaritan was practically staring at us. Somehow he was watching the road and staring at the same time. I saw him notice—I saw his eyes take in Rochelle's blooming Afro. But when he looked at her, when he noticed, I couldn't tell what it was that he saw.

I said, "What kind of jewelry does your wife make?"

He leaned forward, surprised and relieved. He smiled at me in the rearview mirror. "Beads," he said, nodding. "Beads and shells she collects from the beach."

"Nice." I nodded back.

"She's really an artist."

"Mm." I kept nodding.

"Of course, I'm prejudiced."

"Of course," I said.

Now he turned crimson. "I mean, I'm prejudiced because I'm her husband." He glanced again at Rochelle. At Mademoiselle Eugénie.

"Yes," I said.

He tugged at his collar, at his tie. "Don't you think all husbands should be prejudiced in favor of their wives?"

It was like he couldn't stop using the word. "Definitely."

Ma told me once that it was always a bad idea to embarrass men. Always.

Now he kept his eyes on the road. Now he hunched his shoulders, gripped the wheel. I stared at his bulging knuckles. I could see that he was mad at himself.

I felt the tiniest trickle of fear then, at the back of my throat. I wanted to tell Rochelle that at last I understood. I knew what it felt like to be afraid of Whites.

28

I MEAN, ME, ANN AHERN, A GIRL FROM SOUTH BOSTON! Most people that I knew—who grew up where I did—I wanted to tell Rochelle that I'd felt terribly terribly exposed. Sitting there, in the backseat. The thing was, I hadn't known that having feelings for her would leave me open like that. I pictured Rochelle from before. In the car, before, driving with me. Now I knew why she hadn't taken off her clothes. Or at least, I thought I did. I wanted to tell her that I understood why she hadn't let me touch her. Why, back then, she couldn't have taken the chance.

When we sat at the counter in the pancake house—the Good Samaritan had left us in the parking lot; he was not a vengeful man after all—when we three sat on the vinyl stools (we'd already washed ourselves, the dried blood, in the bathroom), I said, under my breath, so only Rochelle could hear: "I understand. I mean, for the first time."

She frowned. She hadn't spoken a word since the Good Samaritan had stopped his car.

Mademoiselle Eugénie excused herself to make a phone call.

Rochelle watched her walk to the phone. Probably Mademoiselle Eugénie was calling Colleen. Probably she was.

Rochelle sighed. She looked beyond tired, beyond defeated. I said, "I mean, before I didn't understand how afraid she must have been." I gestured to Mademoiselle Eugénie. The phone was in the hallway by the front door. She stood with her back to us, eyes downcast, both hands gripping the receiver. "But now I do."

Rochelle raised her eyebrows.

"When you really love someone," I said, as if that was a complete thought.

She kept looking at me.

"I used to have this strange sensation." I shook my head. "I mean, a while ago. Before I met you. I'd see peoples' bodies as separate from them." Her rich brown eyes were wet and shiny. "But not anymore."

She held her face still, immobile.

"To tell the truth, I don't think I've ever felt like that, standing by the side of the road."

"You gonna tell us then?"

"Tell you what?" But as soon as the words were out of my mouth I realized what she was asking. I couldn't believe it. I shook my head.

She shook hers.

"How can you ask me that again?"

"Again has nothing to do with it! Try *still*," she hissed. "I still have to go to that school! I still have to sit with those boys."

"How do you expect me to live? Can you tell me that? Am I gonna come and live in your house, with your crazy aunt? The three of us all cozy!"

She stood up. "This is it, Ann! This is the point where—what else do you want? You say you understand what it feels like. So if you understand, this is the point where you do something different!" She reached both arms up, to cover her head, and it was like her whole body was cringing. "You think you're not like your fat friend. You think you're not like those Southie mothers." She shook her head, her elbows jutting forward. "Here's the thing. I don't care what you *feel*. I care what you *do*!"

I practically jumped off my stool. "See! You just proved my point! How can you not care what I feel?"

She dropped her long arms. "Not like that! I didn't mean it like that."

"You don't care what I feel. And then I'm supposed to rat on some Southie kid. And then you leave. You go off with Jean and her *I Spy* friends." I gestured toward Mademoiselle Eugénie. I was just about to ask, What about me? What about me? Where, in this *I Spy* plan, in this *I Spy* future, where's the place for *me*, when I looked toward the pay phone, and saw that Mademoiselle Eugénie wasn't there.

Rochelle caught the look on my face and turned around. We both scanned the restaurant. Obviously Mademoiselle Eugénie would not be hard to find. The place was half full. It wasn't even six A.M. and the place was half full of White people eating the Big Breakfast. Couples in heavy winter coats. Old people, families. They sat in maple-color captain's chairs at thick wood tables, staring at us. I hadn't noticed them this time, when we'd come in. I was so preoccupied with Rochelle, with wanting to tell her how I felt, that I hadn't noticed them notice us. But of course they had. They did. Now they sat stunned, watching us fight, a Black girl and a White. The polite ones turned back to their pancakes, their French toast. They ate slow, diligent, with their mouths closed. I thought of the time before, just Rochelle and me at the counter, the coffee spurting out her nose and mouth; I searched for the waitress with big boobs—ASK ME WHAT A FUDGEANNA IS—but she wasn't there. I wanted to laugh out loud, like a crazy person. I wanted to laugh and laugh and laugh.

"Wait here," Rochelle said, over her shoulder as she started to move toward the door. As she started to run.

And so I waited. I waited, but already I knew that Mademoiselle Eugénie was gone.

29

After that, we never saw her again. She disappeared. Mademoiselle Eugénie—Jeanie—Jean—walked out of that restaurant and none of us, at least as far as I knew, none of us ever saw her again. In the end, it was hard to accept, like when someone dies: the absolute absence of the physical person. No wonder little kids cry when their mothers walk out of the room. Even if I hated her now, her absolute absence was disconcerting. Was lonely-making.

Sometimes, I liked to imagine her crossing the Bourne Bridge. Which was something she must have done the moment she left the pancake house. She must have passed that desperate sign, ignoring the Samaritans' blue number, and hurried over the bridge. Of course, it's possible she hitched a ride or stowed away in someone's car; maybe she drove, or was driven, rather than walked over that bridge, which would have been more efficient, and which was probably more likely. Still, when I pictured her, I always imagined her on foot: the slender Black body hustling, hustling (she made you think of *action* verbs), hustling over the Bourne Bridge, its giant silver girders bending, graceful, around her. When I tried to hold this image in my mind's eye, I always pictured the bouffant hairdo, the bright, tight French clothes.

It's terrible, I know, that I still liked to imagine her this way—it's dishonest to hold a false picture in my mind—a vivid bird, an oasis, etc.—which was not who she was when she crossed over that bridge. Which was not who she'd ever been. To tell the truth, after all this time, I still didn't know who she was. Not really. Not the way I knew Flynn, say, or even Rochelle. Not the way you know someone you love. But I was pretty certain, no matter what I did or didn't know, Mademoiselle Eugénie wasn't anybody's pleasure but her own.

Did her disappearance mean she'd gone successfully underground? I wasn't sure. I was beginning to wonder whether this *I Spy* business was, if not exactly pretend, then maybe exaggerated. Which was not to say that I thought Mademoiselle Eugénie or Aunt Colleen had made it up. But it occurred to me after the accident, when we were standing helpless on the embankment, it occurred to me that maybe they themselves were not the militants they thought they were. Not the militants they wanted to be. I mean, what militant, *I Spy* thing had they actually done? They went to meetings sure, but what had they actually accomplished?

The thing about *I Spy* groups was that they made the news: the Black Panthers, the Symbionese Liberation Army. And lately, something called the Weather Underground, which sounded strange, if you asked me, what weather underground could there possibly be? But I'm losing my point, which was that if they really were an *I Spy* group, how come I'd never heard of them?

The police never came. The police that had supposedly learned Mademoiselle Eugénie's whereabouts on Cape Cod, they never showed. Rochelle called Big Al and Miriam from the pancake house (she refused to call her aunt), and Big Al came in his stately car. By then we'd been sitting at the counter for more than a couple of hours. We didn't have any money, so we kept asking for another cup of coffee, another cup of tea, in order to postpone paying the bill. The elderly waitress knew something was wrong, but she didn't bother us, didn't once meet our anxious eyes, just kept refilling our cups. Rochelle didn't speak the whole time. She was embarrassed, I think, that Mademoiselle Eugénie had left her behind— more than embarrassed, mortified—and I tried to think of ways to comfort her; I tried to think of encouraging things to say. At some point I told her I was sorry that she didn't have, wouldn't get, the opportunity to prove herself worthy and willing. She tilted her long face in my direction. She said, "Here's a tip. Don't be talking about things you know zero— *zero*—about."

I felt the familiar panic again. To tell the truth, I was finding it hard not to have *nostalgie* for things that were over, past, even for things that hadn't actually been that great. Already, I felt *nostalgie* for every moment I'd spent with Rochelle, even the ones when she'd been incredibly mad at me. When she'd been mad about the Greek goddess of love. I knew it was wrong, perverse maybe, to be homesick for someone who was sitting right there, next to you, and I tried to stop, but could not. Maybe the *I Spy* thing wasn't so much phony, pretend, as it was a kind of *nostalgie* for the 1960s, which were over, done. Maybe Mademoiselle Eugénie and Aunt Colleen and now Rochelle had *nostalgie* for whatever chance or opportunity they'd promised. Whatever incredible transformation. A different life, a different self. Maybe we all just wanted different selves. *My name is Ann Ahern, and I want to go to the cinema.*

Big Al paid our bill and drove us off the Cape. He drove us straight to the hospital. We were surprised—the accident seemed so long ago—but didn't protest. Rochelle sat silent in the passenger seat. Now all the minutes seemed speeded up, short. I knew that soon I would have to leave Rochelle, and so I wanted the time in the car to go incredibly slow. I wanted to look out the window at the passing scenery and talk; I wanted to notice the cranberry bogs, the sea grass, the golden cat-o'-nine-tails; at last, at last, I was interested in what was happening *outside* the car, and I wanted to talk about it with Rochelle, discuss it, the way couples did. But now it was too late; now we were on the interstate; now we were entering the city again; now we were arriving at City Hospital.

Aunt Colleen met us at the door to the emergency room. She was pacing back and forth on the concrete platform where ambulances dropped off patients. Before Big Al even came to a full stop, she opened the passenger door. She looked stricken, the strong brown face distorted with fear. I was wondering how long Rochelle had been living with her when Aunt Colleen pulled Rochelle roughly out of the car. I looked the other way—out of politeness, out of respect for Rochelle—the one thing you never got in the projects was privacy, *privacy*—I ignored the aunt's lunging embrace.

Big Al parked the car. I stayed in the backseat. I didn't want to leave him. He had this reassuring way of moving, like everything going to be all right. He had this reassuring way of accepting you exactly the way you were. For the second time, I had the urge to ask him about the Greek goddess of love and why Rochelle had gotten so angry. But the thing was, by now, I knew the answer myself.

I should have tried harder in the car. That was it: I should have insisted on touching Rochelle. After all, Aphrodite was the goddess of love—of love and beauty and something called rapture. When I tried to picture it, touching Rochelle, all I saw was her angry response. When I pictured lifting Rochelle's shirt—kissing the Black belly—her small, Black breasts—in my mind's eye, all I saw was the black Black skin. An ocean of black. Now in the parking lot of City Hospital, in the backseat of Big Al's cream-colored car, I said to myself, out loud: "I was afraid of getting lost."

Big Al turned and smiled like he knew what on earth I was talking about.

"What's that word mean anyhow? Rapture?"

He draped an arm over the back of the front seat. His eyes were sad, surprised, patient. He nodded like I'd asked a yes or no question. He made that comforting sound again, at the back of his throat. "It means—you could say—just what you said, just now. Getting lost."

He waited patiently outside the car while I wept.

Inside, the emergency room was full of squalling kids. Rochelle and her aunt sat outside the official waiting area, in a crowded hallway, the aunt gripping Rochelle's arm. There were no seats anywhere.

Big Al stood behind me, one of his wide, flat hands resting on my shoulder. "You see anybody yet?"

The aunt shrugged. "Just triage."

Rochelle scratched at the little bits of dried blood still on her fingers.

Big Al said, "Where's that? I'm gonna take Ann in."

The aunt looked through me like I wasn't there.

I said, "Wait."

Big Al dropped his hand.

Rochelle shifted in her seat.

I said, "The thing is, I'm not like Flynn. I'm not like those Southie mothers." My voice was cracking. "How could you even *say* that!"

Rochelle sighed, rubbing her long face with both hands.

"For Christ's sake. I rode the late Black bus!"

Rochelle stared.

"I traveled incog-Negro for you!"

The aunt stood. "Watch your mouth, little girl."

"Doesn't that count? Doesn't that matter?" I stepped

around the aunt. "Like Cousy and Russell!" I started to cry. "I thought, I thought." I squatted down, so I could see her face, the soft brown eyes, the liquid pennies. "I mean, I'd do anything to take it back. I mean, with you, in the car. I wish I had." I sobbed. I tried to get control of my voice. "More than anything, I wish I had!"

Rochelle said, softly, "Ann, you know that's not what this is about."

"I was afraid of getting lost. Is that so hard to understand? Is that a freaking crime?"

Gently, gently, she pulled my hair. "Don't be lying to yourself, Ann. It doesn't suit you."

It was beyond any feeling I had ever felt. Beyond, beyond.

30

The word in French for rapture is *RAVISSEMENT*. The word in French for lost is *perdu*. The word in French for fire is *feu*. Only that was the fire in your fireplace. The fire of sticks, of twigs. Ma used to say, How do you start a fire in the woods? Rub two Boy Scouts together. The word for when your house is on fire was *incendie*. When I was sent to St. Joe's, Sister Gail came and brought me a French/English dictionary so that I could look up all the words. The word in French for gasoline is *essence*. The word in French for fuel is *combustible*. Most people didn't realize but the average home was full of what the fire department called natural *combustibles*. Natural fuels. Nail polish remover. Cough medicine. Anything with *alcool*.

Of course, the house in Jamaica Plain was empty: They were all at the hospital tending Rochelle. I had no trouble getting in. It was strangely comforting to be back in the Black house. There was the front hall table piled high with hats and scarves and gloves. There was the row of rubber boots. I went straight up the stairs, past the Black mirror, past the Black living room, to Mademoiselle Eugénie's bedroom. The word in French for sparse is *épars*.

Sister Gail suggested that while I was at St. Joe's I should write a letter to Mademoiselle Eugénie, even though she'd never get it. She said I should write a letter to Aunt Colleen and Rochelle, to all the people who had disappointed me. Who I had disappointed. Disappointed was the wrong word. The word in French for disappointment is *déception*. The word in French for betrayal is *trahison*. I tried to explain to Sister Gail that I had already written several letters to Mademoiselle Eugénie; that everything that happened that first year of the busing had happened because of those stupid letters. But she said these letters would be different, would be about forgiveness. Theirs and mine. The word in French for forgiveness is *pardon*.

At first when you're learning a foreign language, what seems strange is that a different set of words exists for the things you know. But then, after a while, what seems strange is that so many words are the same, that two entirely different peoples, an ocean apart, would choose the exact same sounds. In the end, what causes the most trouble are the words that sound the same but mean different things: *déception, nostalgie, grâce*.

I sat at Mademoiselle Eugénie's child-sized desk. I realized part of the pleasure of setting fires was that you were doing something beyond words. Beyond speech. The word in French for word is *parole*. At first, when I took out the matches, I just wanted to start a modest fire, a neat fire, right there on the child-sized desk. I opened the slender drawer tucked beneath the table's edge. Inside, I found the see-through paper that she had used to write letters home. At first, it was satisfying, watching the orange flames leap up, snapping the filmy paper away. It burned quickly, immediately, singeing my fingers, one blue piece after the other. I hadn't felt the pleasure of singed fingers since eighth grade. After, when all the paper was burned, I put my fingers in my mouth and sucked at the pulsing heat.

But when the paper was gone, I looked around, dissatisfied. I got up from the chair. The only thing that was easy to burn in that room was the pile of books, but Ma had always said that burning books was a sin. I sat down in the reading chair and looked at the books. Here was another by the Black man with the sad, frog's eyes! On the back cover was a different photograph; in this one, he seemed older, wiser. He wore a mustache. He didn't look quite as unsure. Perhaps now he had gone to Paris, France. Perhaps now he had seen the *arrondissements*. But he still had those unbelievably sad eyes. I turned the book over so I didn't have to look at those sorrowful eyes.

I got up and opened the closet. She'd left two dresses behind. It may sound strange, but I tried one of them on—the mustard-green one with the gold rectangles. It's hard to explain. It's not that I wanted to look like her, act like her, in any way. It's that now I was grief-struck, old.

I went down the hall to the bathroom, in search of a mirror. I put the dress on, right over my clothes, but it was way too tight. I pulled off my sweatshirt, stepped out of my dungarees. The dress had a zipper on the side I couldn't zip. A scooped neck. In the mirror, I looked strange, an impersonation of myself. More like a boy instead of less. The mustard color did not look nice against my skin. For a second, I wondered if Rochelle would prefer me this way, in a dress. I didn't think so.

But just thinking that thought, thinking Rochelle's name, made my skin, my eyes, my mouth burst into flames. These were not flames of embarrassment. I thought it was the worst feeling in the world: wanting someone who did not want you back. The word in French for desire is *désir*.

Right then, I thought of Vivien Leigh and Blanche DuBois. I mean, I hadn't thought of that movie, in a long time. Not since that disastrous day in the movie theater. The very first day of all my troubles. The day which, more than any other, had brought me here, to this very moment, in front of Mademoiselle Eugénie's mirror. I remembered that final scene in the movie where Blanche gets dressed up. She gets dressed up so that they can take her away, to what Stanley calls the nuthouse. She pretends she's going someplace else, but Stanley won't let her pretend. Stanley Kowalski. He's cruel to the sister. All through that whole goddamn movie, he's incredibly cruel. He can't wait for her to leave so that he can make love to Stella. So that he can fuck her.

In the mirror, my face was unbelievably pale. There were circles under the circles under my eyes. Because my face is freckled, I almost always seem to have some color. But now even my freckles seemed drained of blood. I remembered that Blanche DuBois put powder on her face, although she had the whitest possible skin. Which, of course, made me think of Elly. Of Flynn. For a second, I pictured Elly's powdery boobs; I pictured Flynn's disgusted frown. And then, there was Blanche DuBois again, breaking the bottle in half. The nigger knife.

At that moment, I realized something which seemed incredibly obvious, incredibly evident once I thought it, but which had been completely hidden, completely impossible to imagine before: Stanley Kowalski was Black. Not a Pollack, Black. That's why Blanche DuBois broke the bottle in half; that's why she was so upset about Stella marrying Stanley; that's why Stella was so sexually satisfied (the movie's about that: about sexual satisfaction); that's why Blanche was named Blanche, which is the French word for White; it was a kind of clue: Stanley was the opposite; they were in the South, in New Orleans, so the writer had had to hide the fact; had had to disguise it and leave clues; but if you were paying attention at all, you figured it out; you had to be paying attention in order to see these things; but once you did, there wasn't any other way to see: if only you opened your eyes.

I opened my eyes, and there I was in the strange dress. I

took it off. I opened the door to the little cabinet under the sink. I squatted down and emptied the contents on the floor. There were plenty of natural fuels. I didn't want to travel incog-Negro anymore. I did not want to ride in the Negro car all by myself. I doused the dress with bleach.

When the fire department came, the upstairs was what they call fully engaged, and I was downstairs, pulling on my jeans.

Epilogue

I HAVEN'T WRITTEN THE LETTERS OF APOLOGY THAT Sister Gail suggested I write. I haven't written to Rochelle to say, *I'm sorry about your aunt.* How do you say you're sorry for ruining somebody else's life? How do you take responsibility for that?

I'm writing this instead.

The police found what they called incriminating materials in the house in Jamaica Plain. Materials relating to Aunt Colleen's political activities. I had been wrong about the *I Spy* business being pretend. It wasn't pretend at all. Aunt Colleen was part of a militant Black group that wanted to separate from the United States. That wanted to form a separate Black state within the boundaries of the United States. Among the materials found was a firearm, a rifle, which had been packed away in the basement. After the fire department put out the blaze, the police really tore through that house. They opened everything, every box and cupboard; they were thrilled to have the opportunity. They'd been watching the house for years.

Through her lawyer, Aunt Colleen argued that the rifle was ancient, it didn't shoot, she'd kept it only for the appearance of self-protection, for the appearance of self-defense. Besides, she'd said, she was a separatist in theory not in practice; the practice was too demanding, she said, too exhausting. But given the nature of the writings found in the house—mostly manifestos, manifestos and declarations of Black independence—the district attorney didn't see it that way. At her sentencing, he asked the judge to send a message to all the militants in the Boston area. Colleen Washington was sentenced to five years. There's hope she'll be out in three. There's intense expectancy.

Sometimes, I try to understand what happened that first year of the busing in terms of what Dr. McGraugh says about consequence and intention. If I understand his point, the consequence of my burning down the house in Jamaica Plain—it would be more accurate to say, *setting it on fire,* because the truth is, although the fire caught, only the top floor burned— Dr. McGraugh would say the consequence was also my intention. In other words, I lost Rochelle because I wanted to. I burned the house *in order* to lose Rochelle.

To tell the truth, that's awfully hard for me to wrap my head around; that's pretty much impossible for me to accept. In my own mind, I burned the house because I had already lost her. I wouldn't have done it otherwise. But Dr. McGraugh says I'm being stubborn, I'm being, his words, resistant to treatment. Dr. McGraugh comes to St. Joe's once a week. If Ma visited, which she does not, she would say about my stubbornness what she'd said about my father's: You ain't Irish for nothing.

Sister Gail also visits. She's back from wherever it was she went, Alabama or New Mexico; she says Boston is cold now, in comparison. When I told her I was writing this, instead of those letters, she told me confession without penance was simply a form of self-aggrandizement. She also said that penance is not a punishment, it's a gift. A way back to ourselves.

Ma told me once that the difference between Protestants and Catholics is the sacraments in general and confession in particular. She says Protestants confess directly to God, but

Catholics understand the caginess of individual will and so confess instead to the priest, God's witness on earth. She says we all want witnesses, even if we pretend we don't. Even if we hate the idea of telling someone the terrible things we've done, we crave being seen, exposed in that particular way, our ugliness known.

Rochelle's living out of state now, with a different aunt, in the small town that houses the prison where Colleen Washington lives. Rochelle and this new (in fact, old) aunt moved there to be close to Colleen. I call Rochelle on the phone from time to time. (There were seven Washingtons listed in that small town, but only two of the listings were new.) As soon as she realizes it's me, Rochelle hangs up. Sister Gail says I should stop doing this. That I'm bothering Rochelle. She says if the State of Massachusetts knew, I'd be in worse trouble than I already am. How to explain that I couldn't possibly be in worse trouble than I already am?

One time, Rochelle actually spoke before she hung up the phone. One time, she said, "Ann, what is it? What more do you want?"

I told her the thing that Ma said about having witnesses on earth. I told her I was writing it all down.

Her sigh was the sigh of an old person. She told me it was nothing new, what I was doing, nothing special. She said White people were always asking Black people to bear witness to their lives, to their humanity. She said it was the oldest story in the universe, the oldest story in the whole swirling galaxy.

But I think she was just being mean, when she said that. I think she was just trying to punish me.

Acknowledgments

This novel takes as its setting the desegregation of the Boston public schools in 1974. I have attempted to be faithful to the events and spirit of the times, although I have exercised a certain amount of artistic license—for instance, compressing and reordering the time line of desegregation to suit my narrative's demands. Like all novels, it is a work of imagination.

Two exceptional nonfiction books about desegregation in Boston were essential: J. Anthony Lukas's *Common Ground: A Turbulent Decade in the Lives of Three American Families* (Knopf, 1985) and Michael Patrick MacDonald's *All Souls: A Family Story from Southie* (Beacon Press, 1999). Russell Banks's *Rule of the Bone* (HarperCollins, 1995) first brought Ann Ahern into view. Banks's essay "Who Will Tell the People" (in *Harper's Magazine,* June 2000) as well as Jane Smiley's "Say It Ain't So, Huck" (also in *Harper's,* January 1996) were challenging in the best possible ways.

James Baldwin's essays *The Fire Next Time* (Dial Press, 1963) and *Notes of a Native Son* (Beacon Press, 1955) shaped my views on the psychology of racism. Thoughts about Tennessee Williams's *A Streetcar Named Desire* were inspired by diverse readings of the play, including the 1951 film directed by Elia Kazan, the 1991 re-creation/deconstruction *Belle Reprieve* by Split Britches and Bloolips, and reviews by Daniel Mendelsohn (in the *New York Review of Books*) of the Roundabout Theater's 2005 productions of *Streetcar* and *The Glass Menagerie* ("Victims on Broadway," May 26, 2005; "Victims on Broadway II," June 9, 2005).

Thanks are due to archivists and librarians at the Boston Public Library (the main branch as well as the Washington Village Branch Library in Southie), Gay Community News Archives, New York Public Library, Northeastern University Archives and Special Collections, and the Schomberg Center for Research in Black Culture. Thanks to those who facilitated research or granted interviews about their experiences in and around Boston (and other locales) in 1974: John Best, Joan Biren (JEB), Eileen Clancy, Amy Hoffman, Eileen Myles, Ector Simpson, Barbara Smith, Patricia Smith, Roberta Stone, and Elaine Sullivan. Thanks to diligent and generous readers: Lee K. Abbott, Pearl Abraham, Marilyn Brownstein, Patricia Chao, Karin Cook, Joyce Driand, Judith Frank, Jaime Grant, Alan Hoffman, Bill Roorbach, Robyn Selman, Steven Sherrill, Patti Sullivan, Linda Villarosa, Rebecca Wanzo, Ara Wilson, and Jacqueline Woodson.

Thanks to the MacDowell Colony, for time and time again. Thanks to the many writers and artists whom I've encountered there whose work has inspired me; recently, the long-term projects of artists Sandro Del Rosario, *tesoro mio,* Dorota Mytych, and Anna Schuleit were transformative. For financial support during the writing of this book, thanks to the Ludwig Vogelstein Foundation, Money for Women/Barbara Deming Memorial Fund, the Ohio Arts Council, the Rona Jaffe Foundation, and the National Endowment for the Arts.

Thanks to my colleagues in the English Departments of Ohio State University and at Mount Holyoke College, especially Valerie Lee, Melanie Rae Thon, Mary Jo Salter, and Donald Weber. Thanks to Cheryl Wall at Rutgers University, who reintroduced me to Baldwin.

Gratitude to generous friends who afforded space for writing: Jacqueline Woodson and Juliet Widoff, Lisa Florman, Steve and Ruth Melville, and Lisa Henderson. Thanks to steadfast Sloan Harris at ICM and dreamy Alexis Gargagliano at Scribner. Bottomless thanks to three readers who intervened at critical junctures (read: moments of abject despair): Karin Cook, Judith Frank, and Patti Sullivan. And to Jaime, who never despairs.

Thanks to Ara, who challenged me to think harder, which turned out to be the greatest gift. And thanks to Ara, Jojo, and Augusta, whose confidence and support are absolute and unconditional, and, therefore, life-sustaining.

A SCRIBNER
READING GROUP GUIDE

MAP OF IRELAND

BY STEPHANIE GRANT

DISCUSSION QUESTIONS

1. *Map of Ireland* opens with an epigraph by the Greek philosopher Heraclitus: "Geography is fate." How does this apply to Ann Ahern? Is she able to escape her geography or her fate in the novel?

2. Ann says, "If I was a certain kind of person, I'd blame my troubles on the desegregation itself. I'd blame my being stuck here on those stupid yellow buses and the violence they seemed to bring" (p. 4). Which characters in *Map of Ireland* would blame their troubles on desegregation? Do you think Ann takes personal responsibility for her crime? Why or why not?

3. Consider Ann's family situation. What kind of example does each parent set for Ann? Who, if anyone, in Ann's life serves as a positive role model?

4. Ann rants silently, "The sixties are over . . . you missed it, don't you realize?" (p. 42) How does the year 1974 influence Ann's attitude? What about Rochelle's? If the revolutionary energy of the 1960s continued into the 1970s, when did the sixties really end? Is there a particular moment in American history that signals or represents that end to you?

5. Ann explains to Mademoiselle Eugenie, "'They say I have a face like the map of Ireland. . . . You can tell where I'm from just by looking at my face'" (p. 60). Why do you suppose Grant chose to name the novel after this line about Ann's appearance? Why does Mademoiselle Eugenie laugh when she compares her face to the map of France?

6. In considering the French word "*nostalgie,*" or "homesickness," Ann states, "'I think I have *nostalgie* for South Boston before the busing'" (p. 61). What do you think Ann means? Do you think her "homesickness" is genuine? What is the difference between homesickness and nostalgia?

7. Twice Rochelle tells Ann, "'I got a short attention span'" (pp. 102, 133), referring to basketball and her last relationship. Do you think Rochelle's meaning changes when she repeats this statement?

8. Ann thinks, "Maybe you always loved the person or people who taught you to speak" (p. 147). Who in this novel helps Ann find her voice?

9. Rochelle teases Ann by telling her she is "traveling incog-Negro." What does this expression mean to Rochelle? What does it mean to Ann?

10. What do you think motivates Ann to set the fire in Mademoiselle Eugenie's bedroom? She explains, "Dr. McGraugh would say the consequence was also my intention. . . . I burned the house *in order* to lose Rochelle. . . . In my own mind, I burned the house because I had already lost her" (p. 192). Which interpretation do you believe, Dr. McGraugh's or Ann's? Why?

11. Throughout the novel Ann is very conscious of Rochelle's race. When is Rochelle conscious of Ann's? How does that consciousness reveal itself?

12. In the scene in the hospital, Ann pleads with Rochelle to stay friends. Why does Rochelle refuse her? Why does Ann think Rochelle refuses her?

13. In chapter 30, Ann comes to a startling realization about the film she saw earlier in the novel, *A Streetcar Named Desire*. "Stanley Kowalski was Black." How does Ann's realization relate to the idea of "traveling incog-Negro"?

14. In the 1970s, desegregation in Northern states was necessary not because segregation was written into law as it was in the American South (separate but equal) but because Northern neighborhoods were segregated and most students went to their neighborhood school. How does this pattern of segregation relate to the title *Map of Ireland*?

15. *Map of Ireland* is a coming-of-age novel. Does it remind you of any other coming-of-age novels you have read? Which ones? Does it differ in any interesting ways?

16. How does Ann's Catholicism structure the novel?

17. What does Sister Gail mean when she tells Ann that "confession without penance is simply a form of self-aggrandizement"?

18. There are a lot of different (literal) maps referred to in the novel. Can you list them?

Enhance Your Book Club

1. Can your book club speak Boston slang? Using the "Wicked Good Guide to Boston English" at http://www.boston-online.com/glossary/ab/index.html, make a set of note cards with definitions of Boston-based words. Have your book club take turns guessing what each slang word means!

2. Schedule a screening of *A Streetcar Named Desire* after your book club meeting. Do members of your book club agree with the interpretation of the characters Stanley, Blanche, and Stella that appears in *Map of Ireland*?

3. Find a map of eastern Massachusetts, either in an atlas or printed from the Internet, and share it with your book club. Trace the routes that Ann travels throughout the novel, from South Boston (http://www.cityofboston.gov), to Jamaica Plain, to the Bourne Bridge, to Provincetown, and back.

4. Ann's world expands when she visits Provincetown, Massachusetts, with Rochelle. Plan your book group's own fantasy vacation to this Cape Cod resort town! If your book club were to visit Provincetown, where would you stay? What sights would you want to see? You can research Provincetown tourism at http://www.provincetowntourismoffice.org.

About the Author

Stephanie Grant's first novel, *The Passion of Alice*, was longlisted for Britain's Orange Broadband Prize for Fiction and was a finalist for the Lambda Literary Award for Best Lesbian Fiction. Her writing has received numerous awards including a fellowship from the National Endowment for the Arts, an Ohio Arts Council Grant, and a Rona Jaffe Foundation Writers' Award. She has taught creative writing at Rutgers University, Ohio State University, and was a Writer-in-Residence at Mount Holyoke College. She is currently Visiting Writer at the Franklin Humanities Institute at Duke University.